r

N

J

.

A long time ago in a galaxy far, far away....

STAR

DARTH

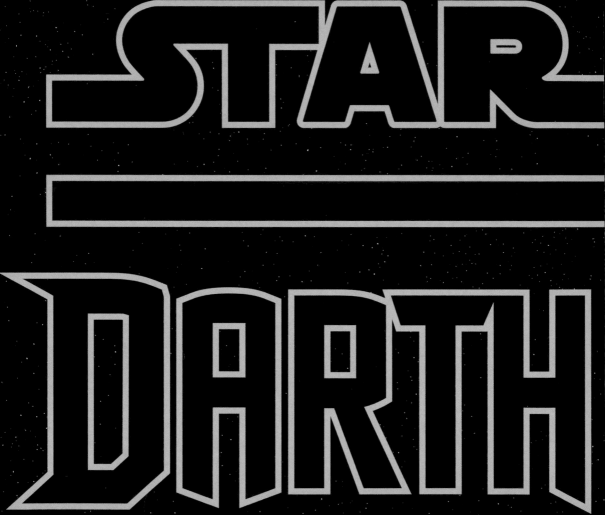

WARS®

VADER

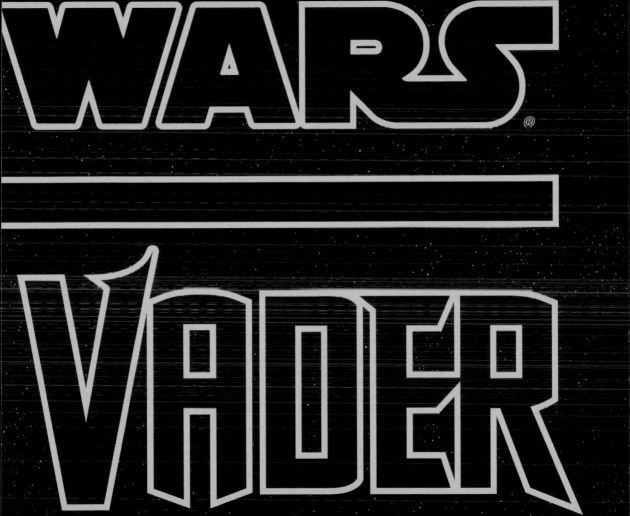

ABDOPUBLISHING.COM

Reinforced library bound edition published in 2017 by Spotlight,
a division of ABDO, PO Box 398166, Minneapolis, Minnesota 55439.
Spotlight produces high-quality reinforced library bound editions for
schools and libraries. Published by agreement with Marvel Characters, Inc.

Printed in the United States of America, North Mankato, Minnesota.
042016
092016

THIS BOOK CONTAINS
RECYCLED MATERIALS

STAR WARS © & TM 2016 LUCASFILM LTD.

PUBLISHER'S CATALOGING IN PUBLICATION DATA

Names: Gillen, Kieron, author. | Larroca, Salvador ; Delgado, Edgar, illustrators.
Title: Vader / by Kieron Gillen ; illustrated by Salvador Larroca and Edgar Delgado.
Description: Minneapolis, MN : Spotlight, [2017] | Series: Star Wars : Darth Vader
Summary: Follow Vader straight from the ending of A New Hope into his own solo
    adventures-showing the Empire's war with the Rebel Alliance from the other
    side! When the Dark Lord needs help, to whom can he turn?
Identifiers: LCCN 2016932362 | ISBN 9781614795209 (v.1 : lib. bdg.) | ISBN
    9781614795216 (v. 2 : lib. bdg.) | ISBN 9781614795223 (v. 3 : lib. bdg.) | ISBN
    9781614795230 (v. 4 : lib. bdg.) | ISBN 9781614795247 (v.5 : lib. bdg.) | ISBN
    9781614795254 (v. 6 : lib. bdg.)
Subjects: LCSH: Vader, Darth (Fictitious character)--Juvenile fiction. | Star Wars
    fiction--Comic books, strips, etc.--Juvenile fiction. | Graphic novels--Juvenile
    fiction.
Classification: DDC 741.5--dc23
LC record available at http://lccn.loc.gov/2016932362

Spotlight

A Division of ABDO
abdopublishing.com

VADER: VOLUME 1

It is a period of insurgence. Rebel spaceships, striking from a hidden base on a moon of Yavin, have won a shocking surprise victory against the rightful reign of the Galactic Empire.

The Empire's ultimate peacekeeping force, THE DEATH STAR, was destroyed due to an unforeseen design flaw. Without this deterrent, the rule of law is in danger. Chaos looms!

For the nineteen years after the vanquishing of the Jedi and his painful rebirth on volcanic Mustafar, Sith Lord DARTH VADER has faithfully served his master. But now, he has failed the Emperor and must pay the price....

KIERON GILLEN
Writer

SALVADOR LARROCA
Artist

EDGAR DELGADO
Colorist

VC's JOE CARAMAGNA
Letterer

ADI GRANOV
Cover Artist

CHARLES BEACHAM
Assistant Editor

JORDAN D. WHITE
Editor

C.B. CEBULSKI &
MIKE MARTS
Executive Editors

AXEL
ALONSO
Editor In Chief

JOE
QUESADA
Chief Creative Officer

DAN
BUCKLEY
Publisher

For Lucasfilm:
Senior Editor JENNIFER HEDDLE
Creative Director MICHAEL SIGLAIN
Lucasfilm Story Group RAYNE ROBERTS, PABLO HIDALGO,
LELAND CHEE

Disney | LUCASFILM

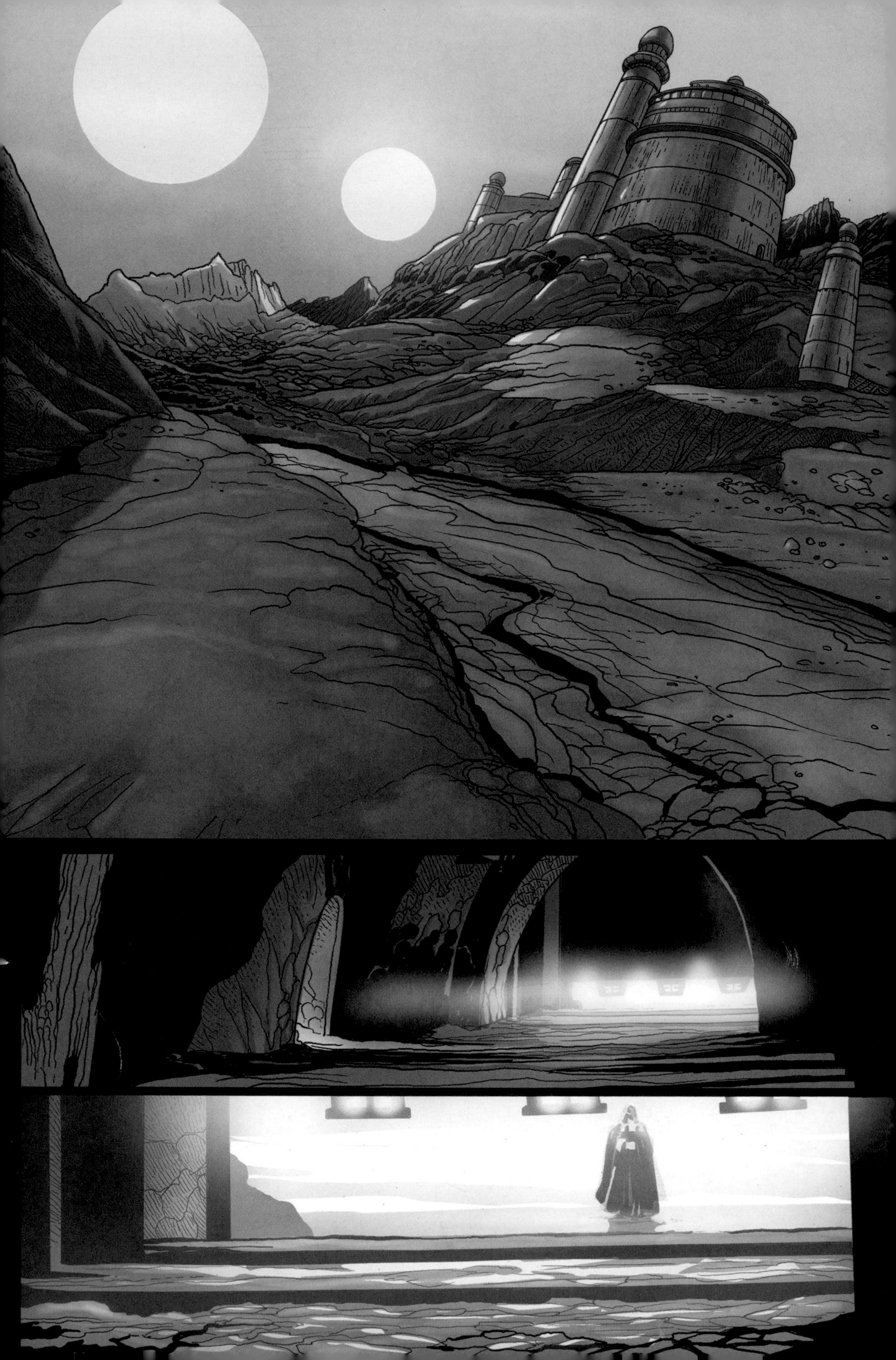

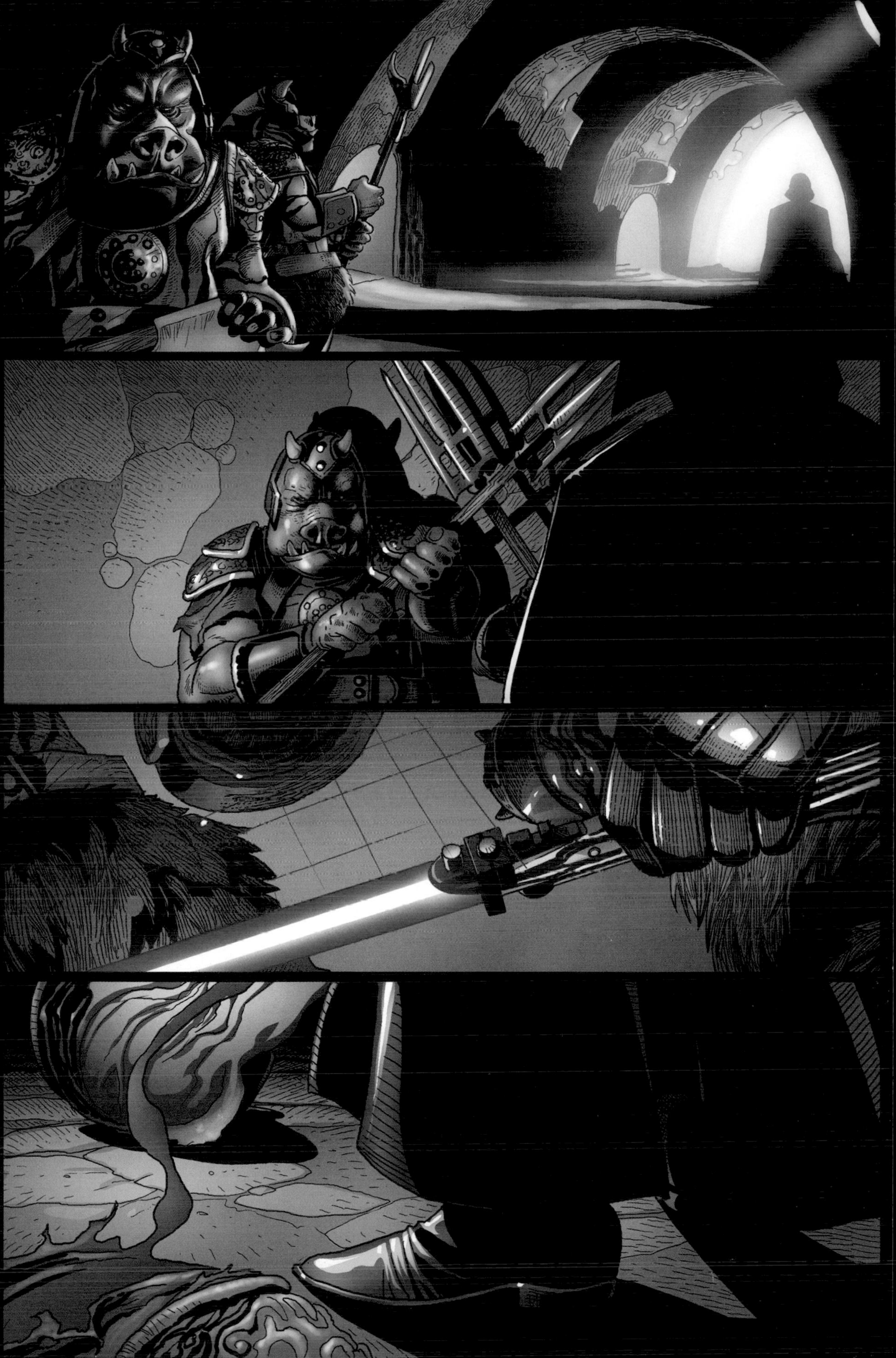

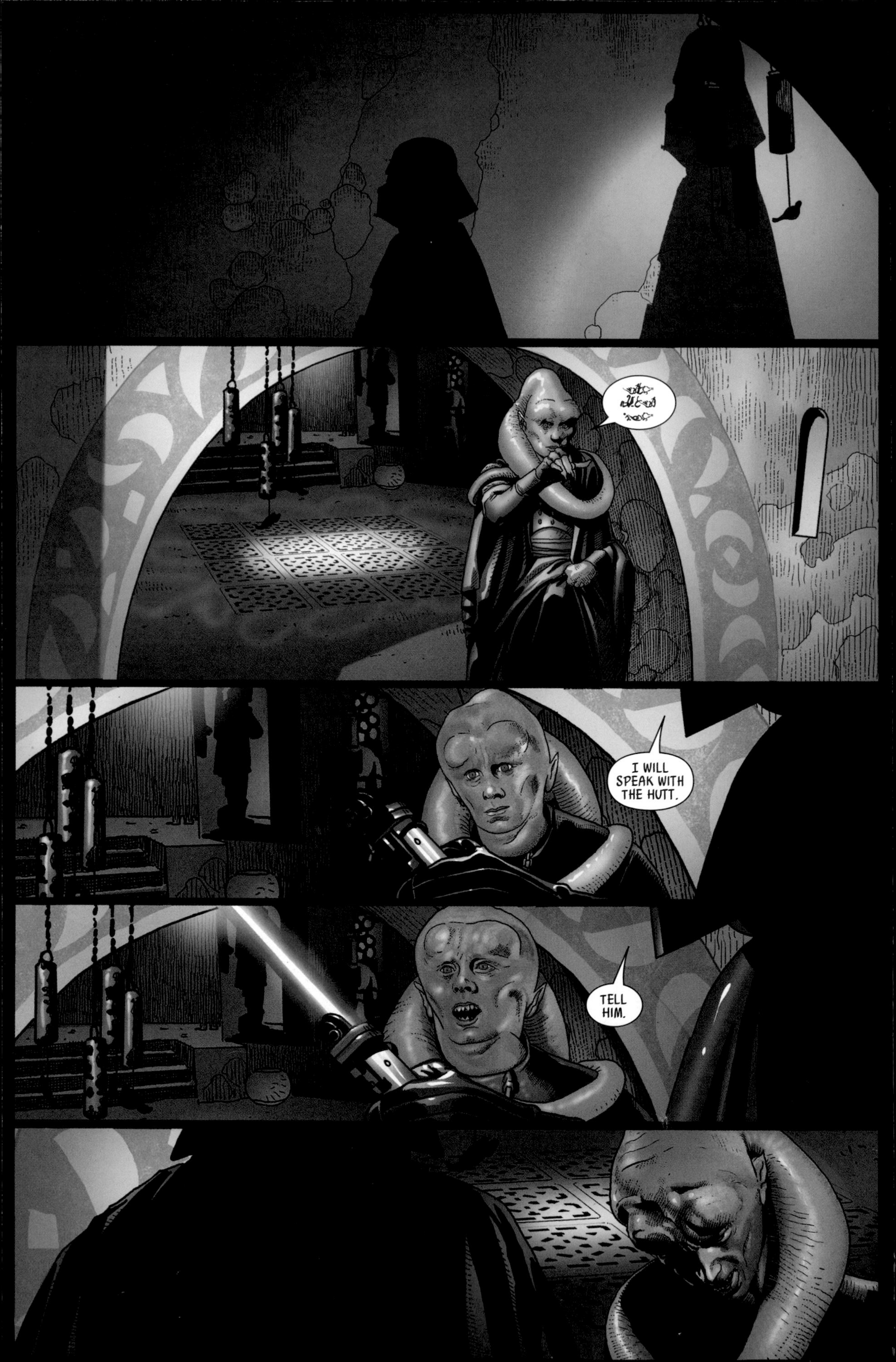
I WILL SPEAK WITH THE HUTT.
TELL HIM.

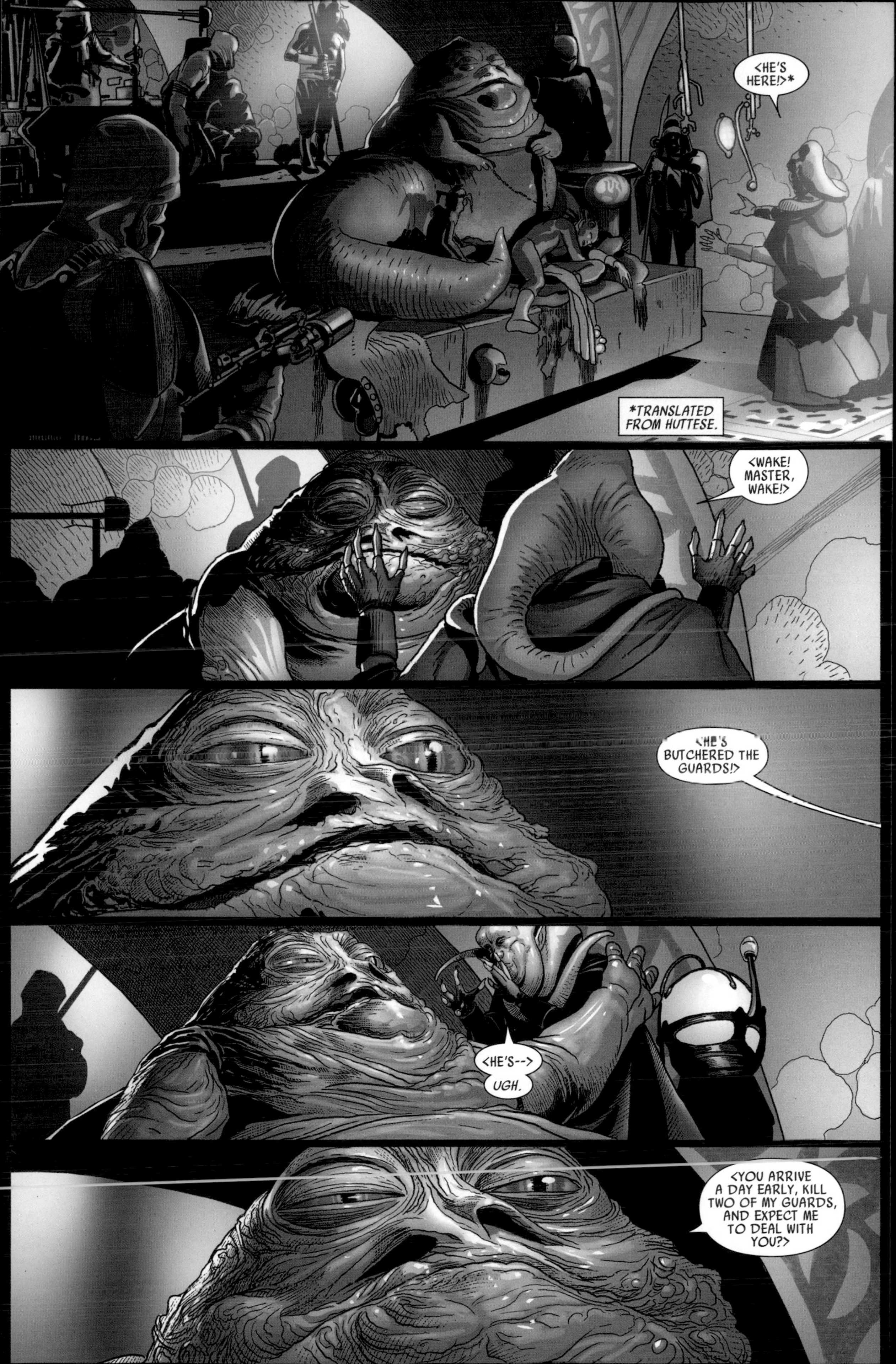

<HE'S HERE!>*
*TRANSLATED FROM HUTTESE.
<WAKE! MASTER, WAKE!>
<HE'S BUTCHERED THE GUARDS!>
<HE'S-->
UGH.
<YOU ARRIVE A DAY EARLY, KILL TWO OF MY GUARDS, AND EXPECT ME TO DEAL WITH YOU?>

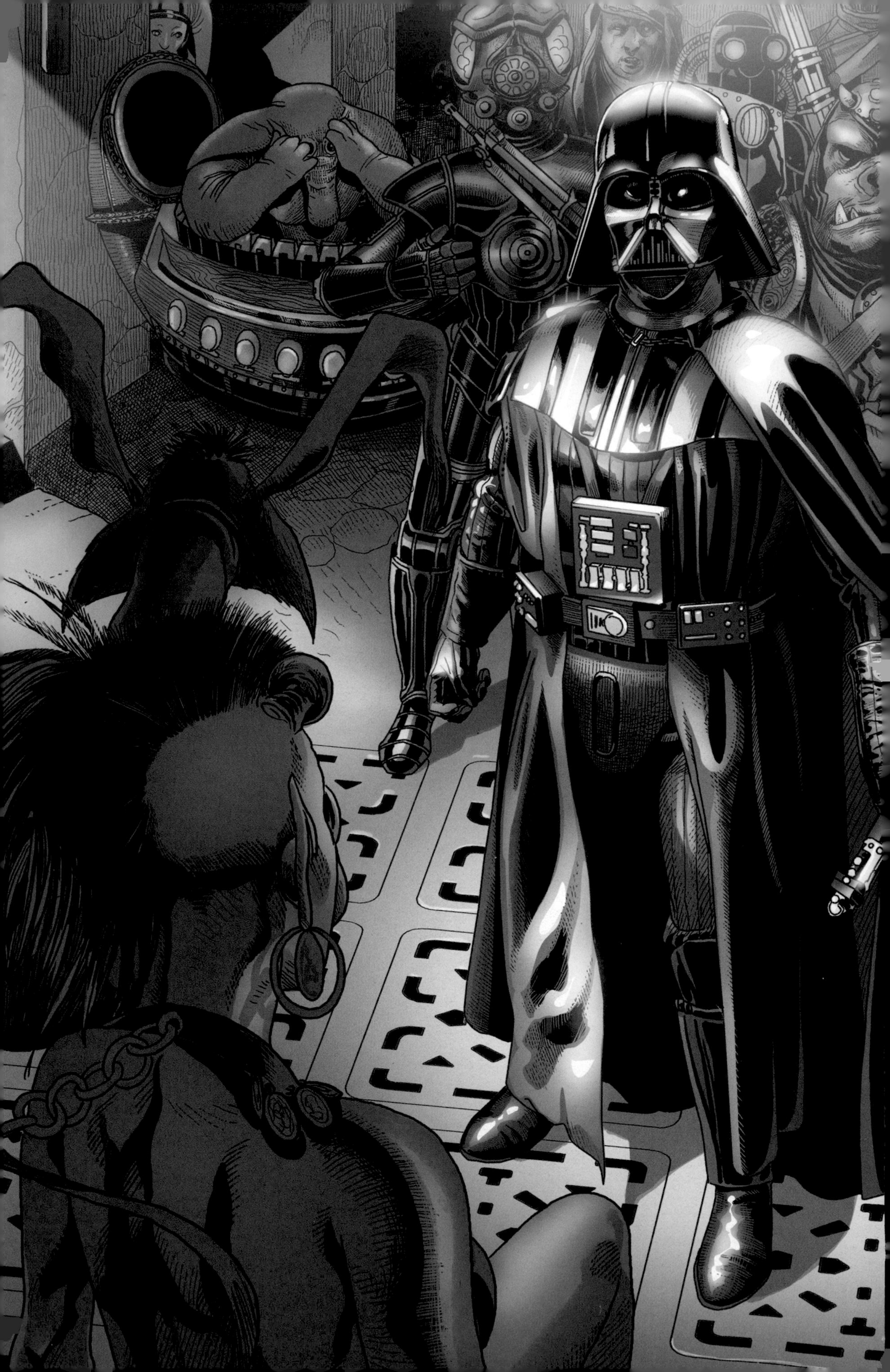

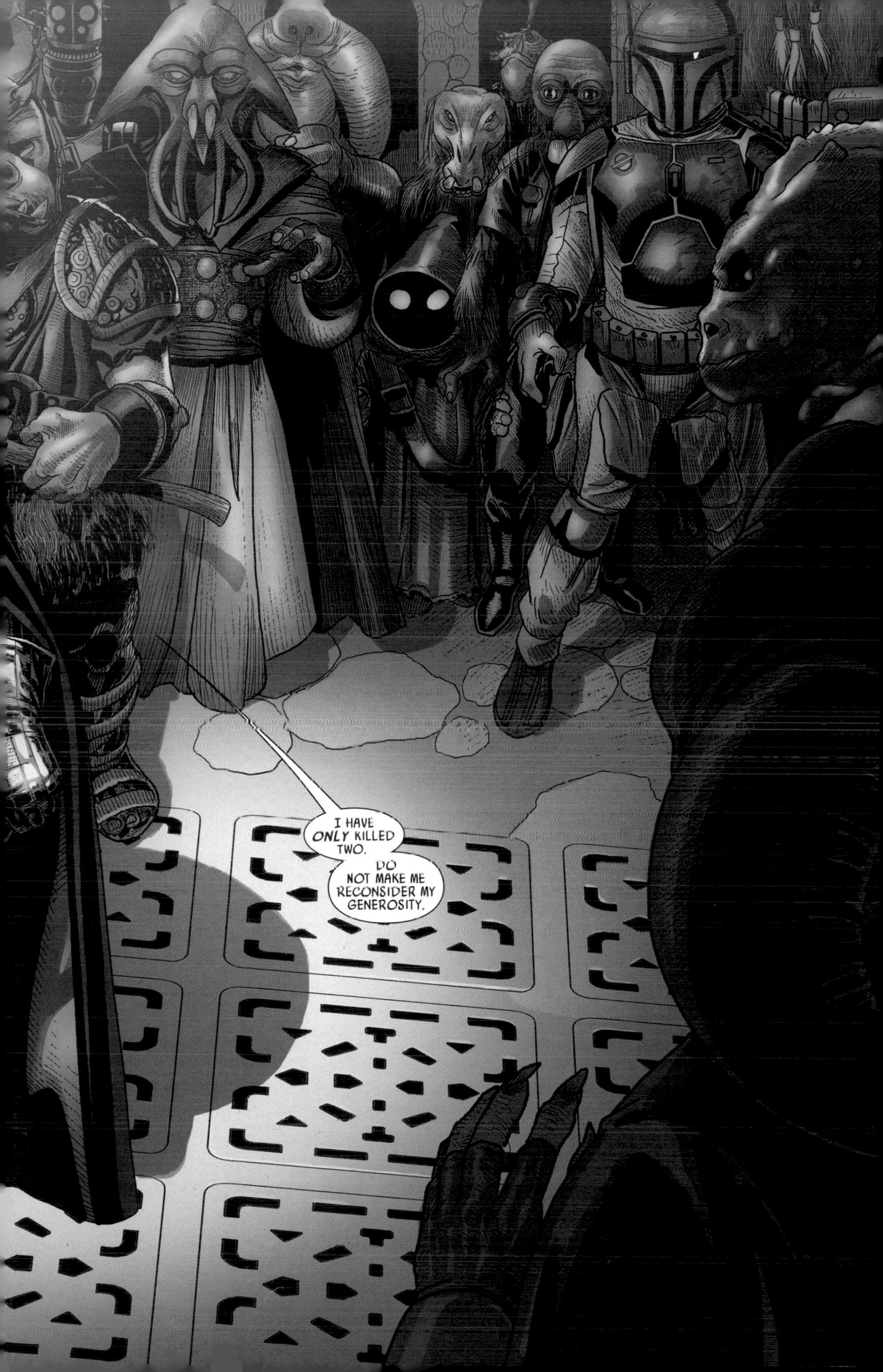
I HAVE ONLY KILLED TWO.
DO NOT MAKE ME RECONSIDER MY GENEROSITY.

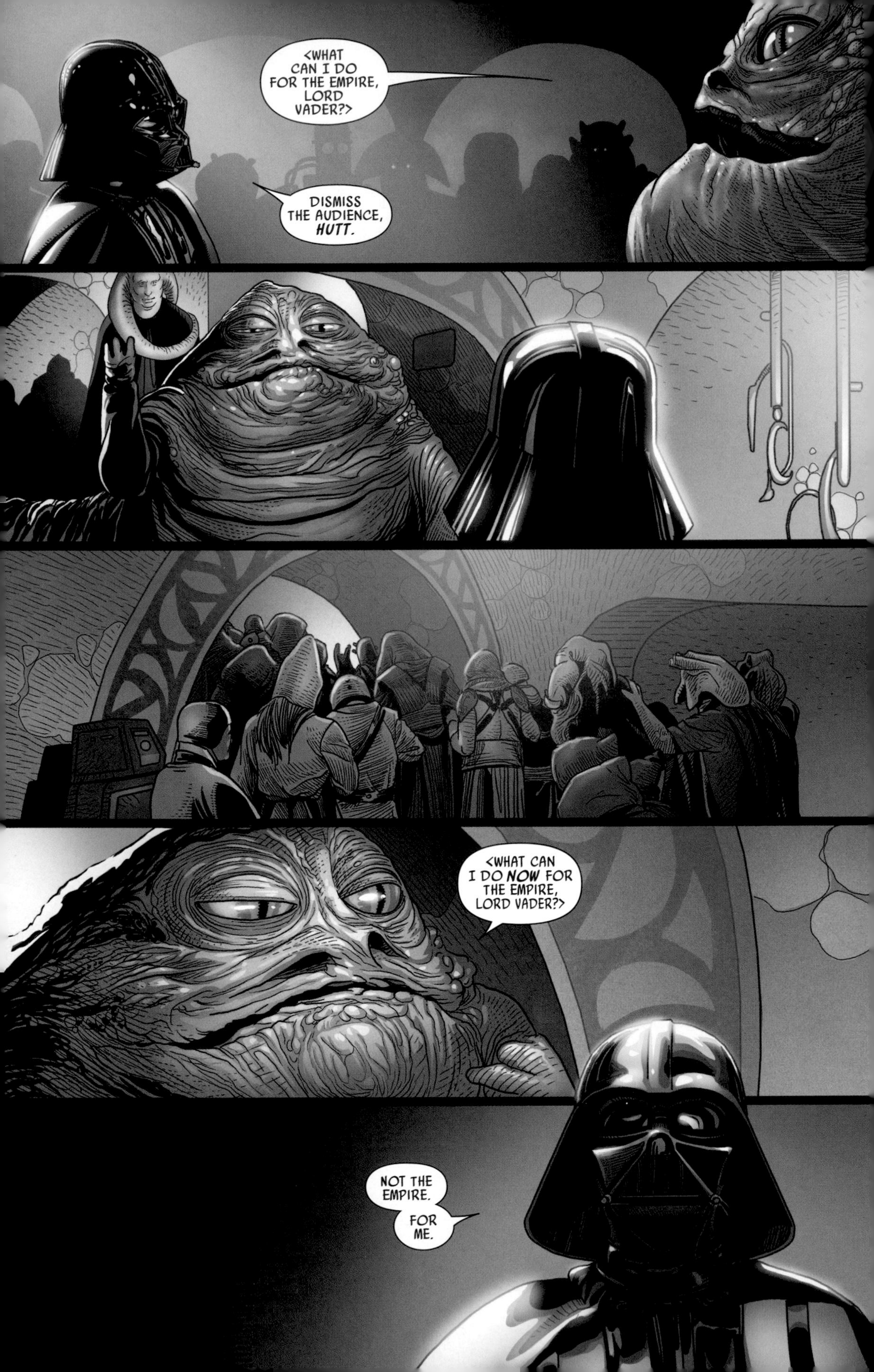

<WHAT CAN I DO FOR THE EMPIRE, LORD VADER?>
DISMISS THE AUDIENCE, *HUTT.*
<WHAT CAN I DO *NOW* FOR THE EMPIRE, LORD VADER?>
NOT THE EMPIRE.
FOR ME.

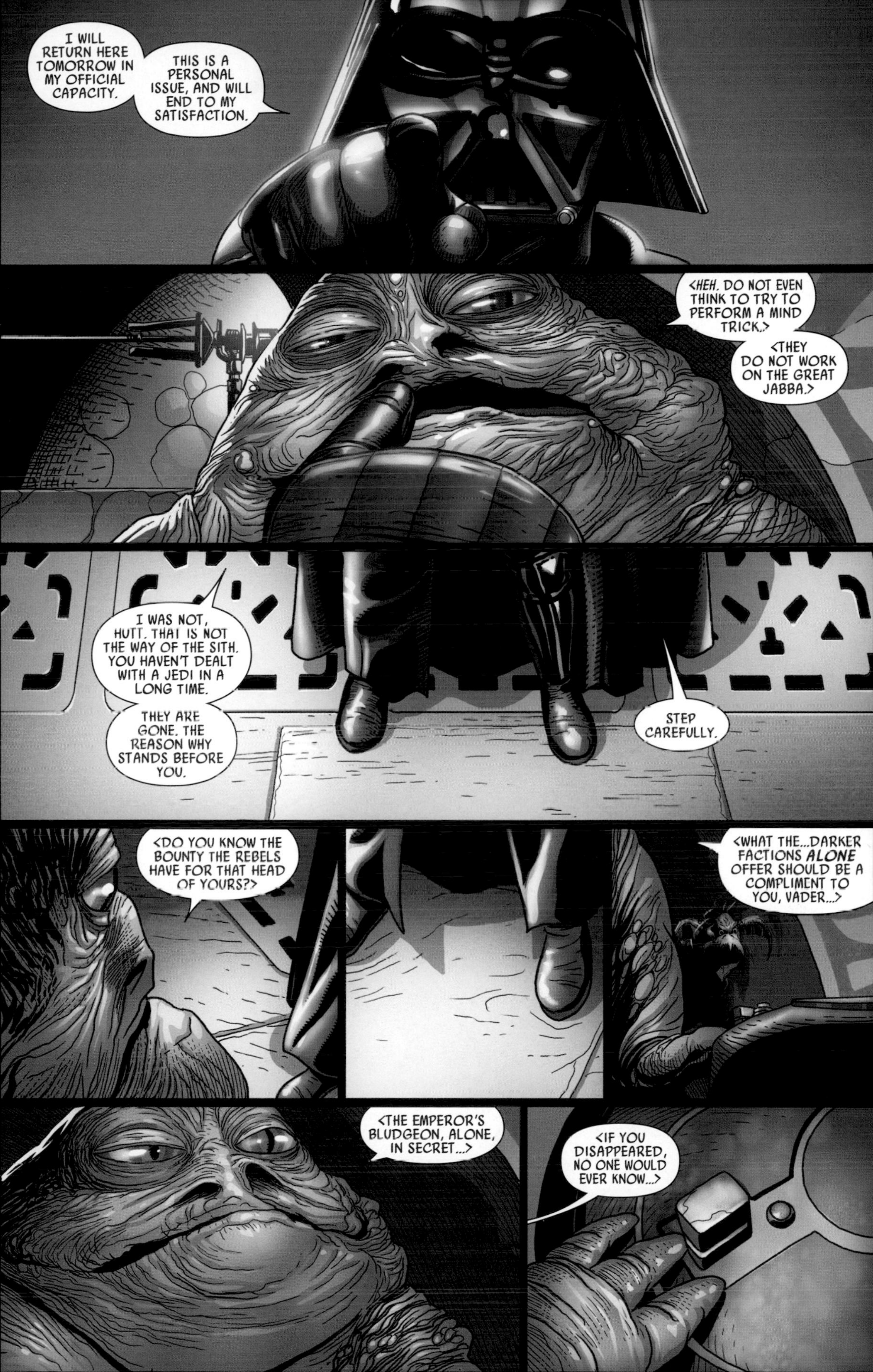
I WILL RETURN HERE TOMORROW IN MY OFFICIAL CAPACITY.
THIS IS A PERSONAL ISSUE, AND WILL END TO MY SATISFACTION.
<HEH. DO NOT EVEN THINK TO TRY TO PERFORM A MIND TRICK.>
<THEY DO NOT WORK ON THE GREAT JABBA.>
I WAS NOT, HUTT. THAT IS NOT THE WAY OF THE SITH. YOU HAVEN'T DEALT WITH A JEDI IN A LONG TIME.
THEY ARE GONE. THE REASON WHY STANDS BEFORE YOU.
STEP CAREFULLY.
<DO YOU KNOW THE BOUNTY THE REBELS HAVE FOR THAT HEAD OF YOURS?>
<WHAT THE...DARKER FACTIONS *ALONE* OFFER SHOULD BE A COMPLIMENT TO YOU, VADER...>
<THE EMPEROR'S BLUDGEON, ALONE, IN SECRET...>
<IF YOU DISAPPEARED, NO ONE WOULD EVER KNOW...>

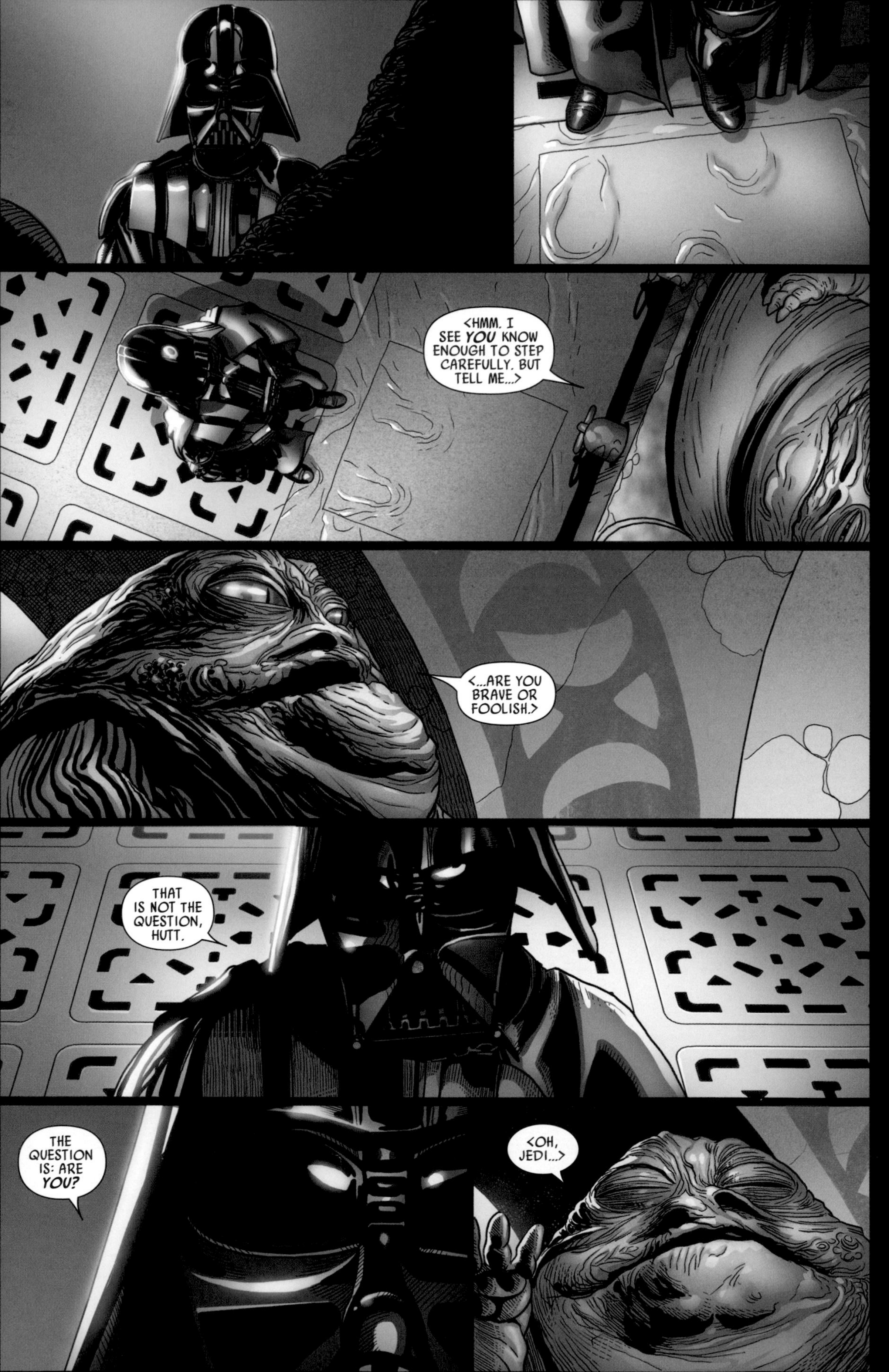
<HMM. I SEE *YOU* KNOW ENOUGH TO STEP CAREFULLY. BUT TELL ME...>
<...ARE YOU BRAVE OR FOOLISH.>
THAT IS NOT THE QUESTION, HUTT.
THE QUESTION IS: ARE *YOU*?
<OH, JEDI...>

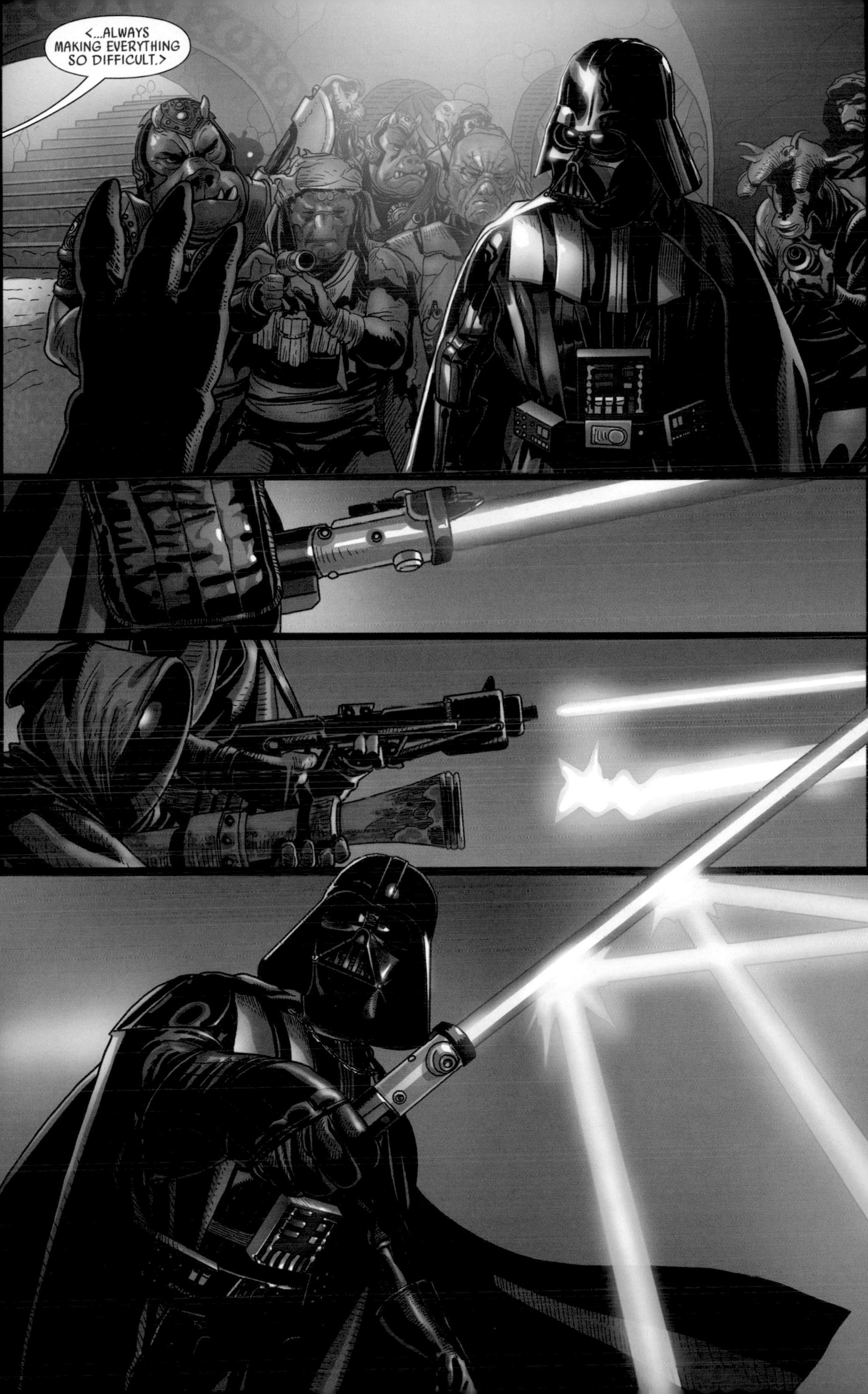
<...ALWAYS MAKING EVERYTHING SO DIFFICULT.>

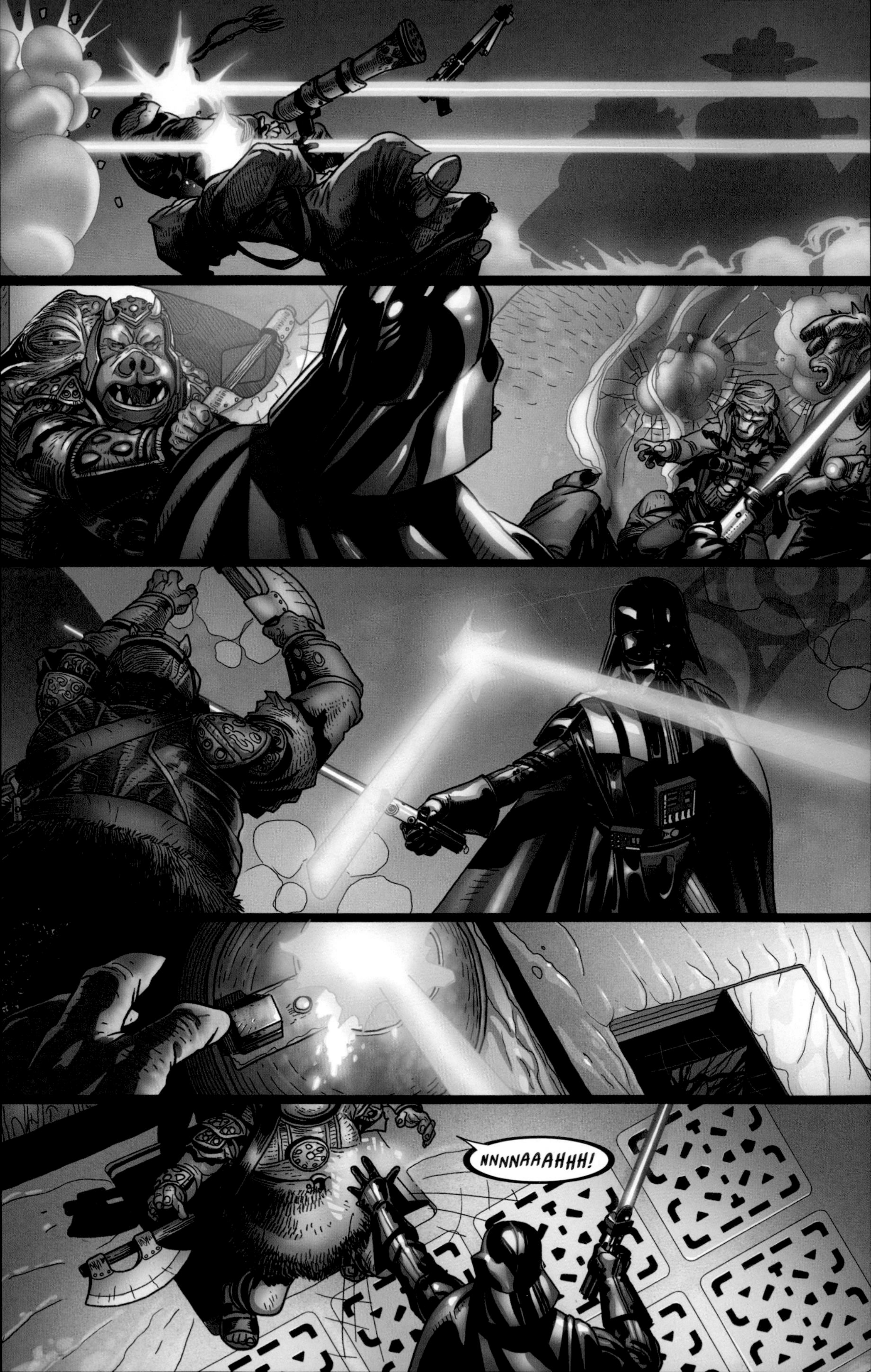
NNNNAAAHHH!

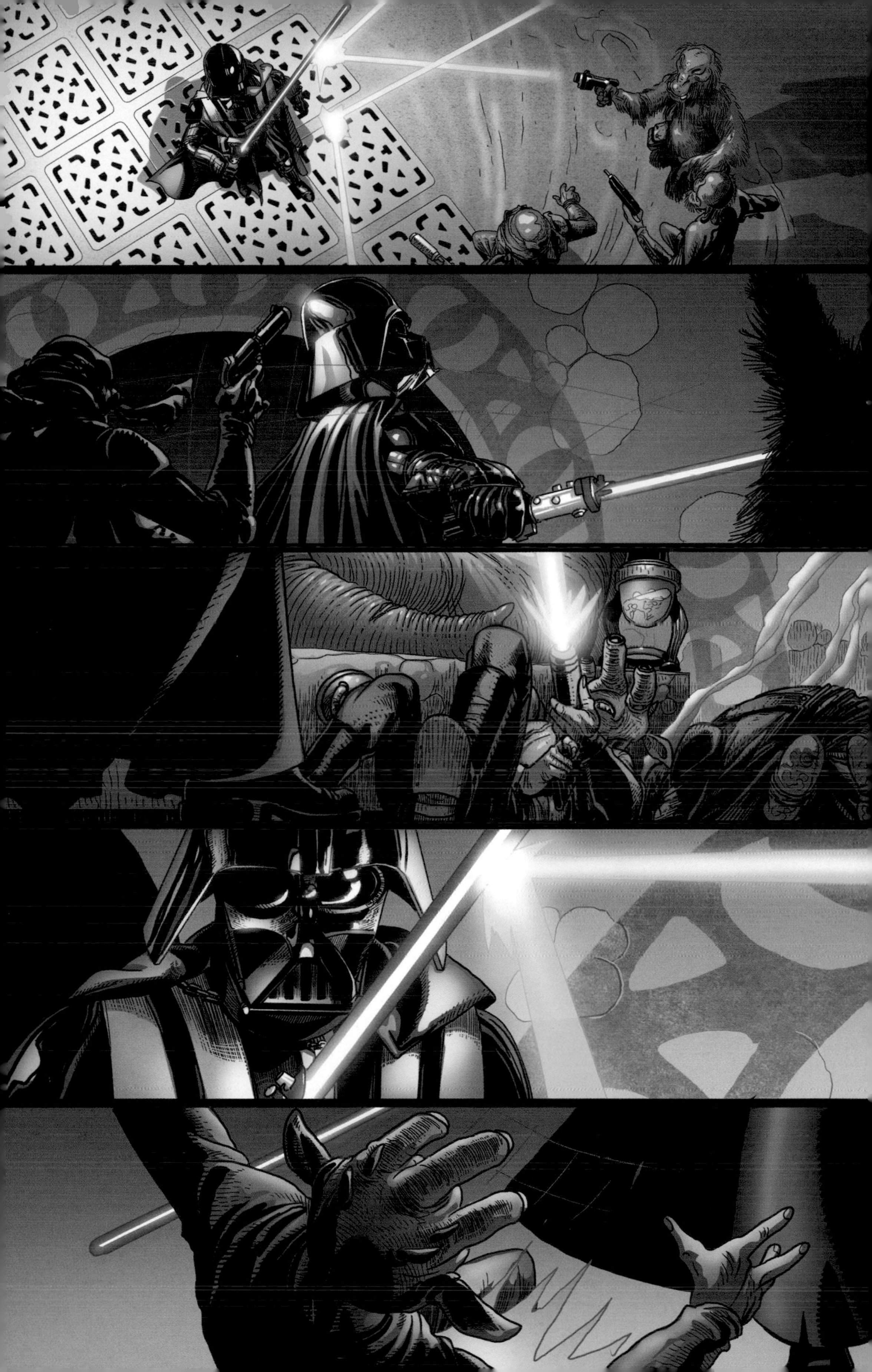

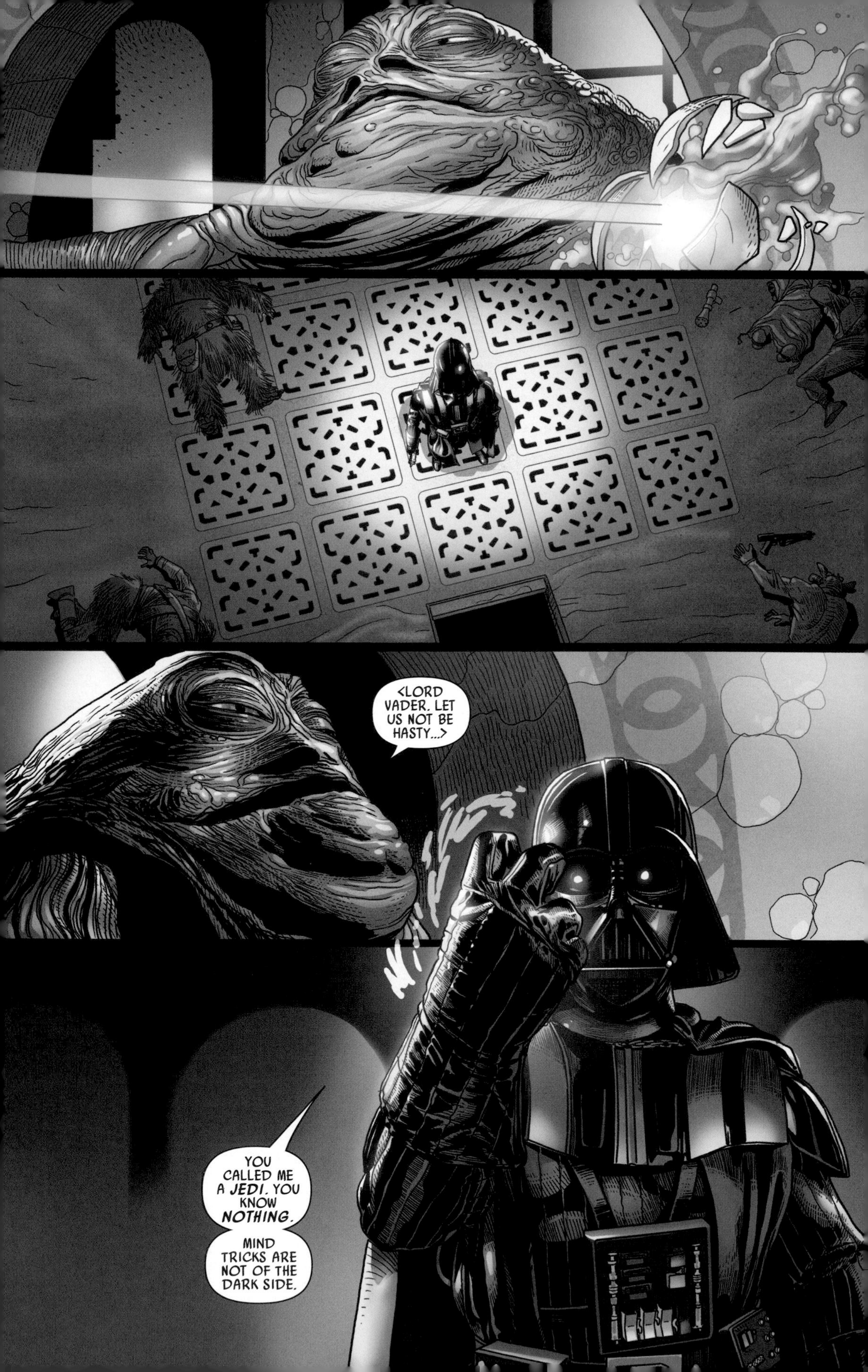
<LORD VADER. LET US NOT BE HASTY...>
YOU CALLED ME A JEDI. YOU KNOW NOTHING.
MIND TRICKS ARE NOT OF THE DARK SIDE.

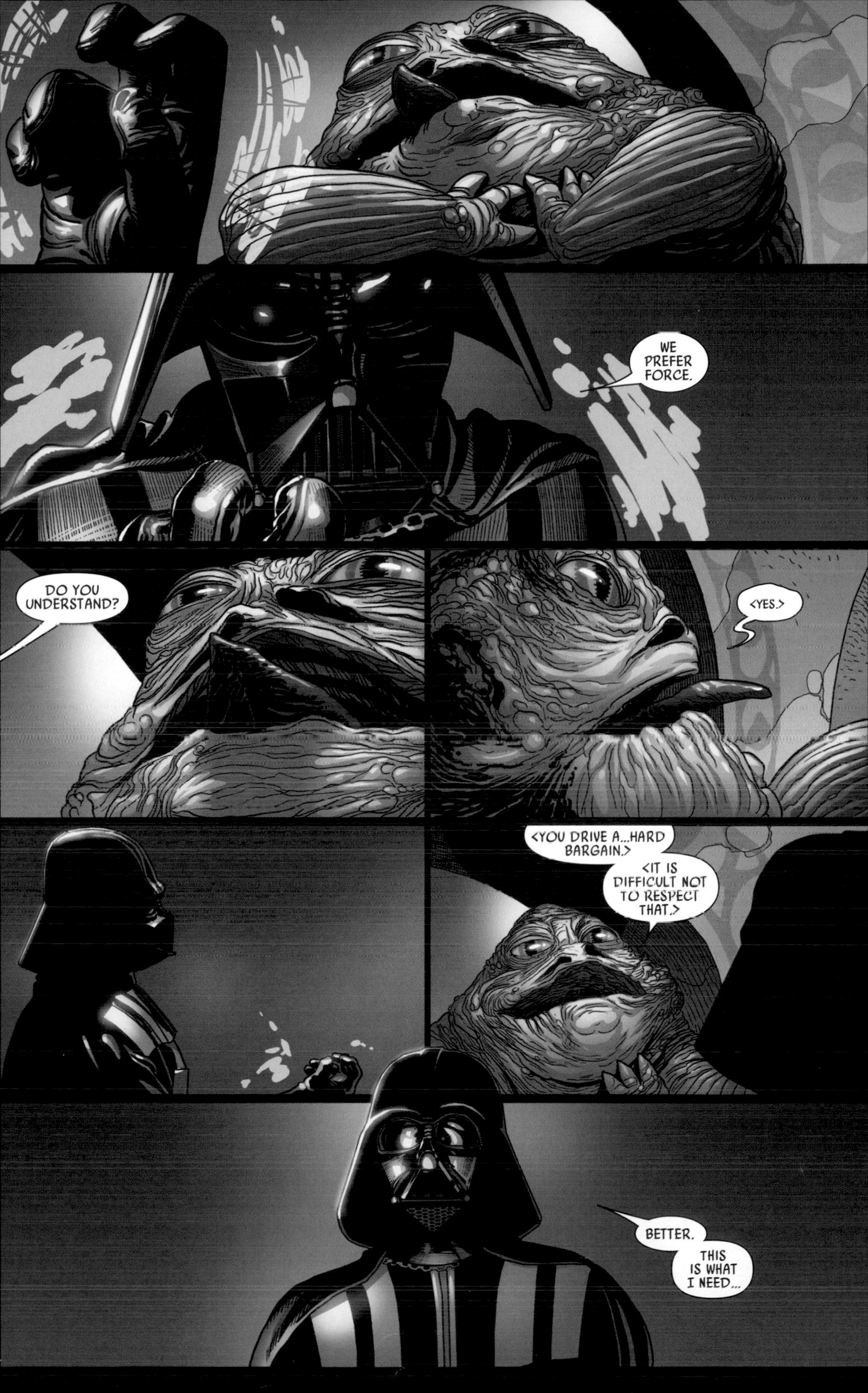
WE PREFER FORCE.
DO YOU UNDERSTAND?
<YES.>
<YOU DRIVE A...HARD BARGAIN.>
<IT IS DIFFICULT NOT TO RESPECT THAT.>
BETTER.
THIS IS WHAT I NEED...

One Day Earlier
The Imperial Palace, Coruscant

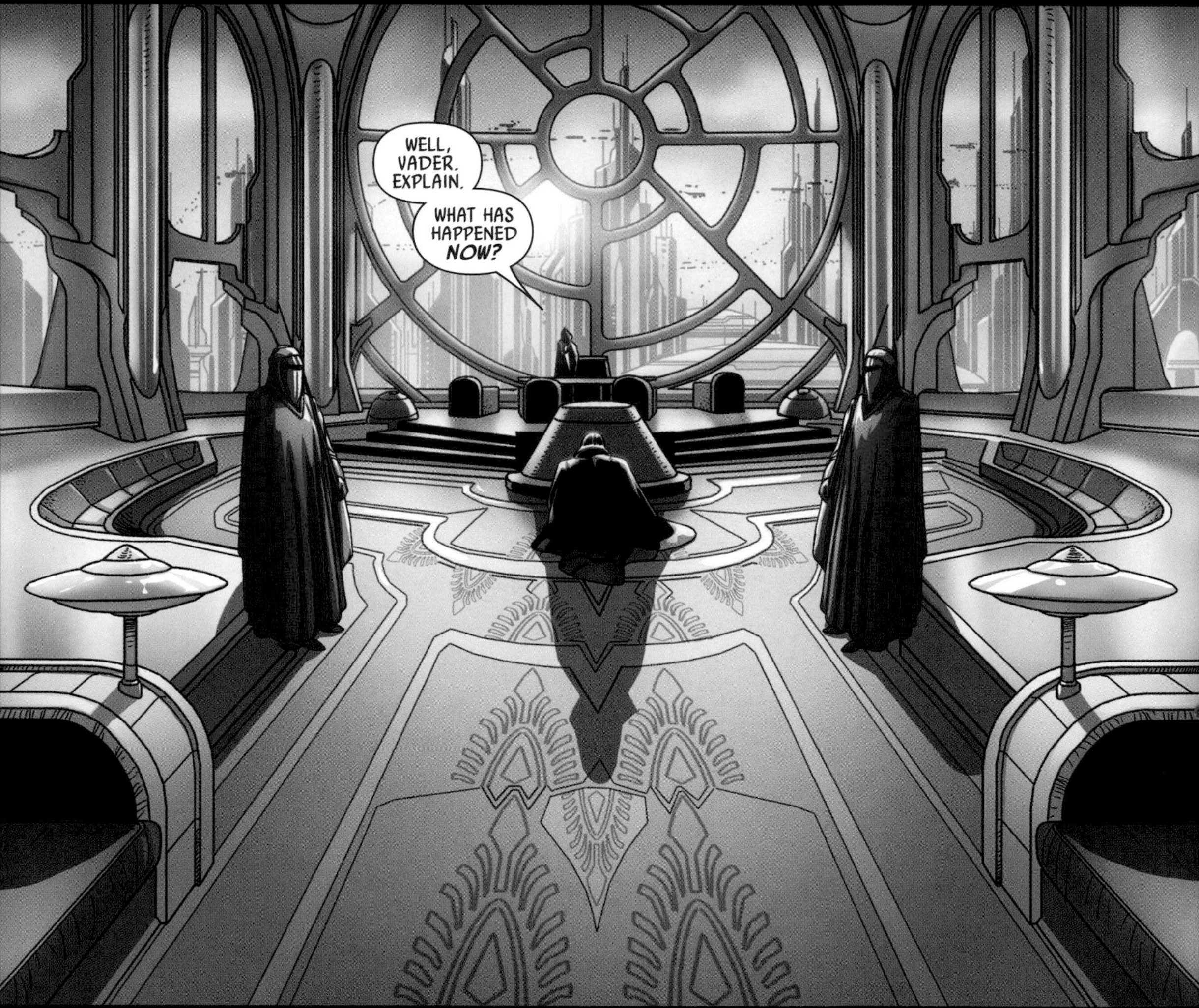
WELL, VADER. EXPLAIN.
WHAT HAS HAPPENED NOW?

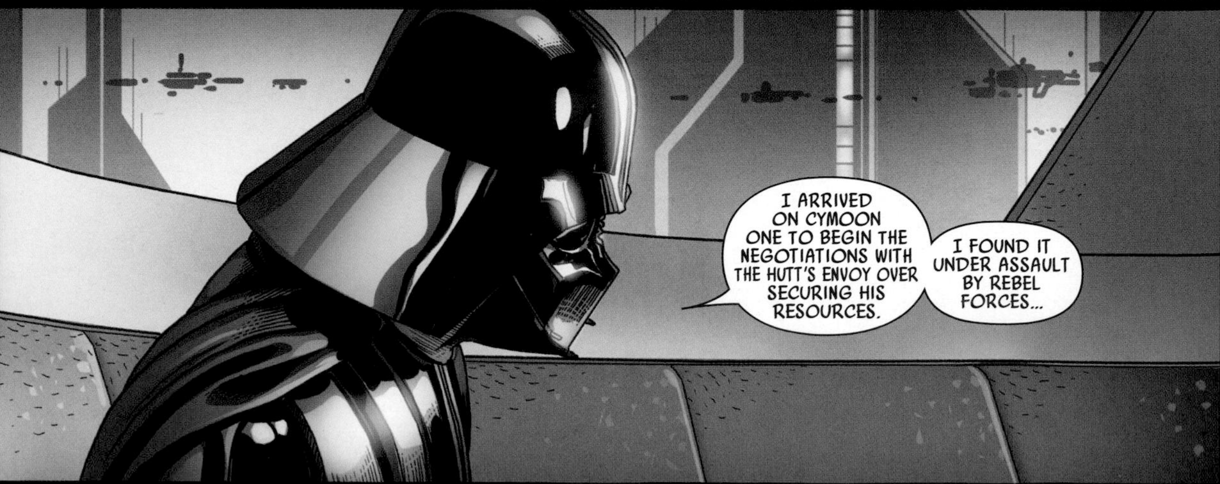
I ARRIVED ON CYMOON ONE TO BEGIN THE NEGOTIATIONS WITH THE HUTT'S ENVOY OVER SECURING HIS RESOURCES.
I FOUND IT UNDER ASSAULT BY REBEL FORCES...

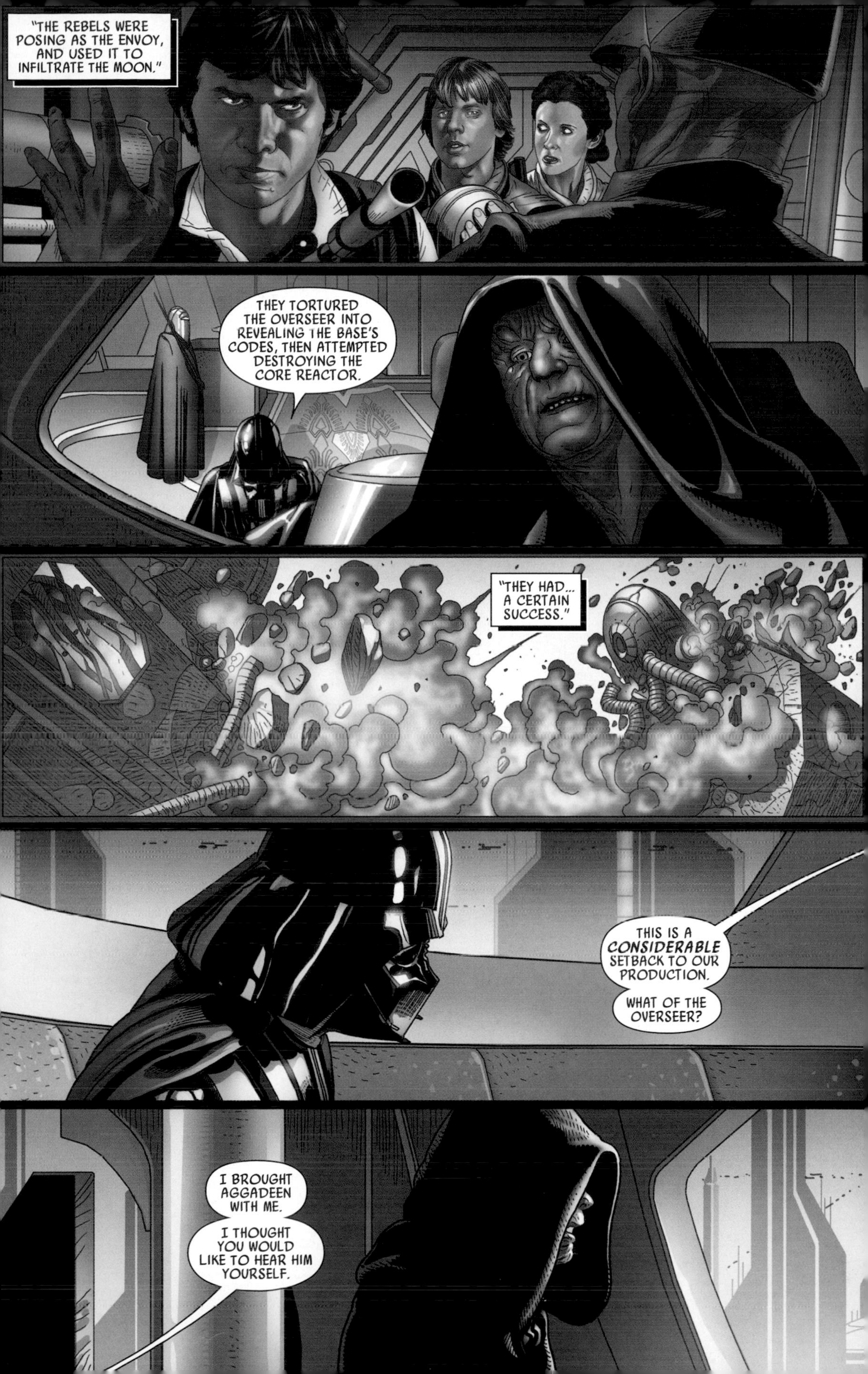
"THE REBELS WERE POSING AS THE ENVOY, AND USED IT TO INFILTRATE THE MOON."
THEY TORTURED THE OVERSEER INTO REVEALING THE BASE'S CODES, THEN ATTEMPTED DESTROYING THE CORE REACTOR.
"THEY HAD... A CERTAIN SUCCESS."
THIS IS A *CONSIDERABLE* SETBACK TO OUR PRODUCTION.
WHAT OF THE OVERSEER?
I BROUGHT AGGADEEN WITH ME.
I THOUGHT YOU WOULD LIKE TO HEAR HIM YOURSELF.

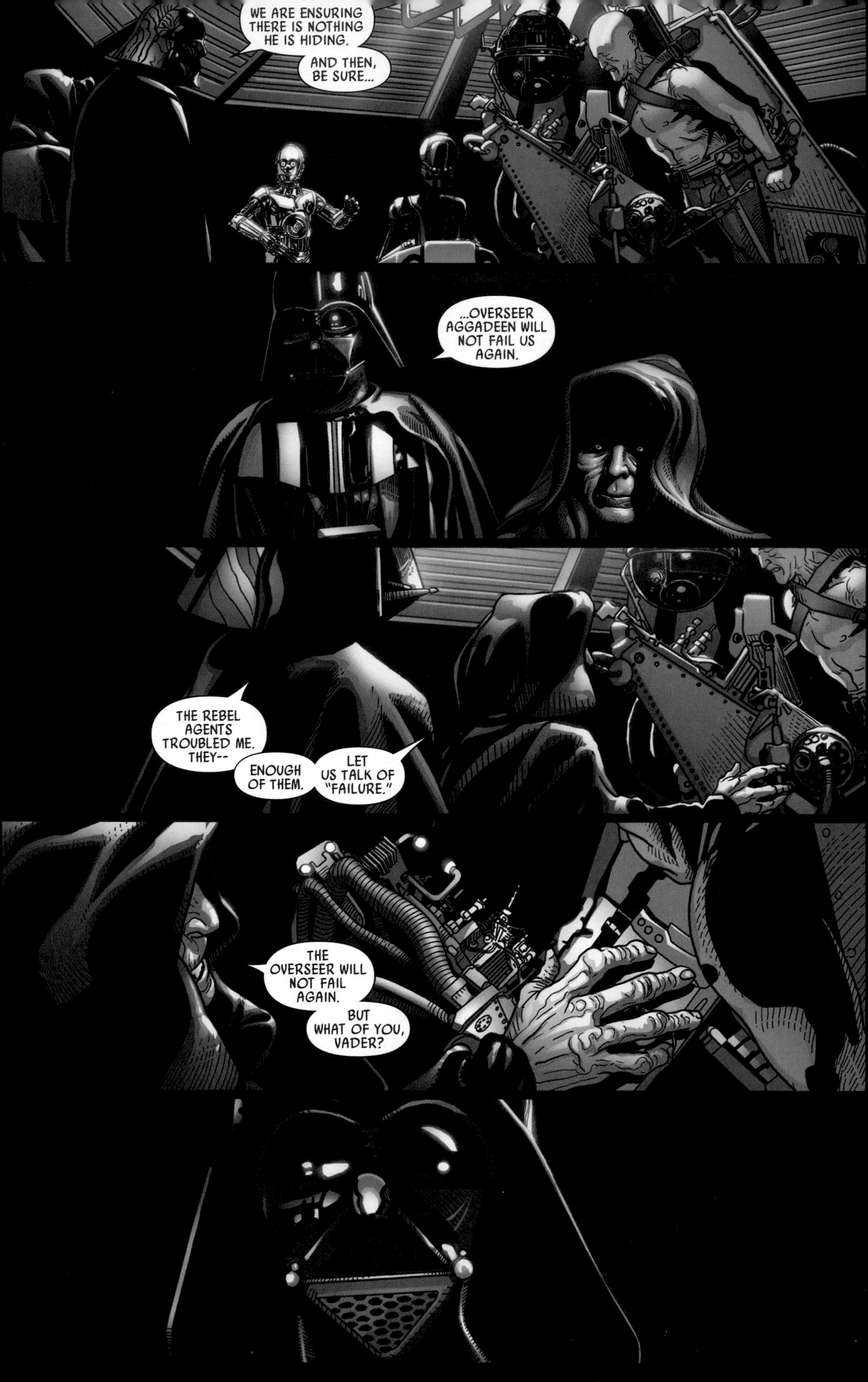

WE ARE ENSURING THERE IS NOTHING HE IS HIDING.
AND THEN, BE SURE...
...OVERSEER AGGADEEN WILL NOT FAIL US AGAIN.
THE REBEL AGENTS TROUBLED ME. THEY--
ENOUGH OF THEM.
LET US TALK OF "FAILURE."
THE OVERSEER WILL NOT FAIL AGAIN.
BUT WHAT OF YOU, VADER?

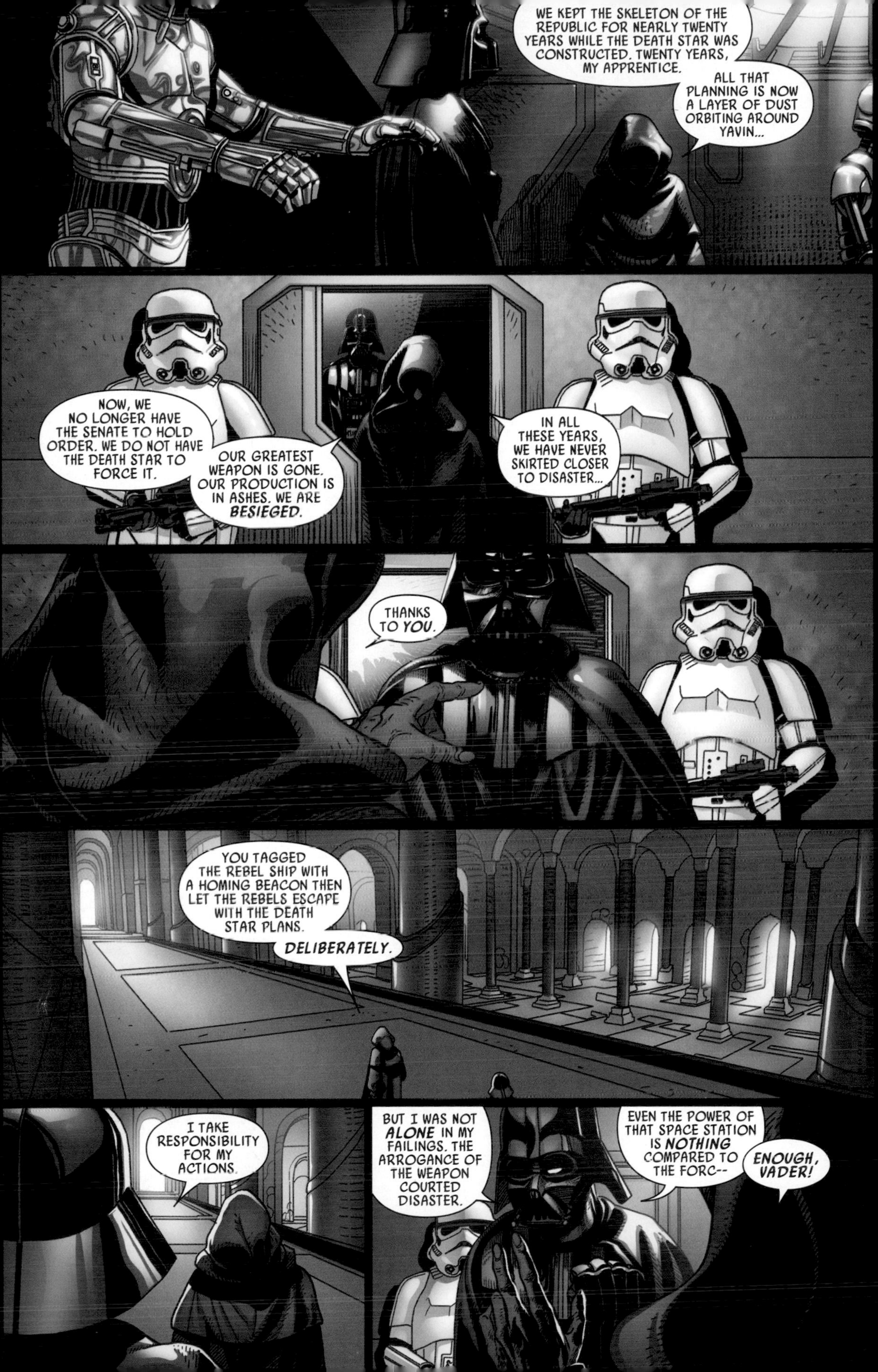
WE KEPT THE SKELETON OF THE REPUBLIC FOR NEARLY TWENTY YEARS WHILE THE DEATH STAR WAS CONSTRUCTED. TWENTY YEARS, MY APPRENTICE.
ALL THAT PLANNING IS NOW A LAYER OF DUST ORBITING AROUND YAVIN...
NOW, WE NO LONGER HAVE THE SENATE TO HOLD ORDER. WE DO NOT HAVE THE DEATH STAR TO FORCE IT.
OUR GREATEST WEAPON IS GONE. OUR PRODUCTION IS IN ASHES. WE ARE BESIEGED.
IN ALL THESE YEARS, WE HAVE NEVER SKIRTED CLOSER TO DISASTER...
THANKS TO YOU.
YOU TAGGED THE REBEL SHIP WITH A HOMING BEACON THEN LET THE REBELS ESCAPE WITH THE DEATH STAR PLANS.
DELIBERATELY.
I TAKE RESPONSIBILITY FOR MY ACTIONS.
BUT I WAS NOT ALONE IN MY FAILINGS. THE ARROGANCE OF THE WEAPON COURTED DISASTER.
EVEN THE POWER OF THAT SPACE STATION IS NOTHING COMPARED TO THE FORC--
ENOUGH, VADER!

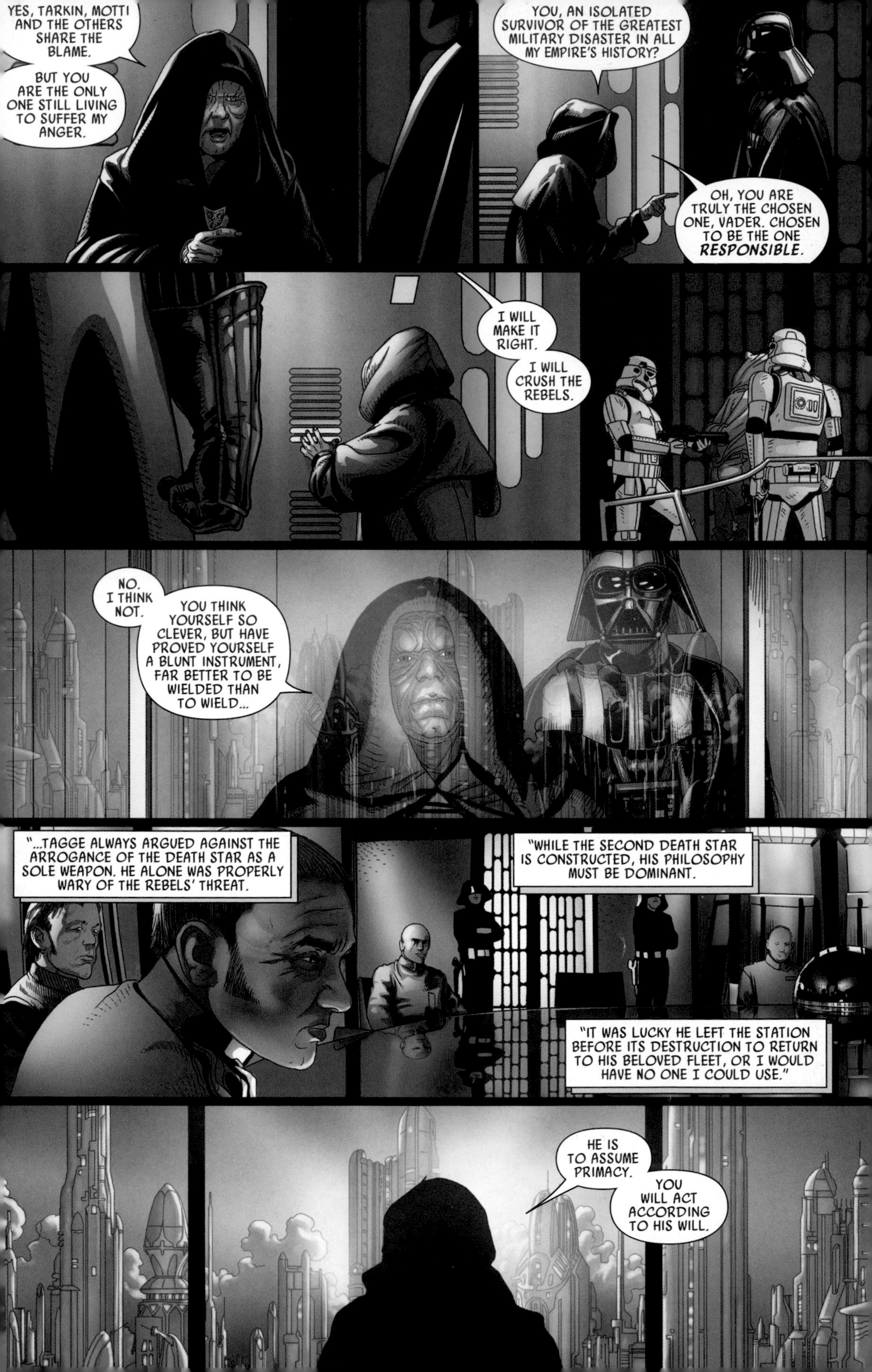
YES, TARKIN, MOTTI AND THE OTHERS SHARE THE BLAME.
BUT YOU ARE THE ONLY ONE STILL LIVING TO SUFFER MY ANGER.
YOU, AN ISOLATED SURVIVOR OF THE GREATEST MILITARY DISASTER IN ALL MY EMPIRE'S HISTORY?
OH, YOU ARE TRULY THE CHOSEN ONE, VADER. CHOSEN TO BE THE ONE RESPONSIBLE.
I WILL MAKE IT RIGHT.
I WILL CRUSH THE REBELS.
NO. I THINK NOT.
YOU THINK YOURSELF SO CLEVER, BUT HAVE PROVED YOURSELF A BLUNT INSTRUMENT, FAR BETTER TO BE WIELDED THAN TO WIELD...
"...TAGGE ALWAYS ARGUED AGAINST THE ARROGANCE OF THE DEATH STAR AS A SOLE WEAPON. HE ALONE WAS PROPERLY WARY OF THE REBELS' THREAT.
"WHILE THE SECOND DEATH STAR IS CONSTRUCTED, HIS PHILOSOPHY MUST BE DOMINANT.
"IT WAS LUCKY HE LEFT THE STATION BEFORE ITS DESTRUCTION TO RETURN TO HIS BELOVED FLEET, OR I WOULD HAVE NO ONE I COULD USE."
HE IS TO ASSUME PRIMACY.
YOU WILL ACT ACCORDING TO HIS WILL.

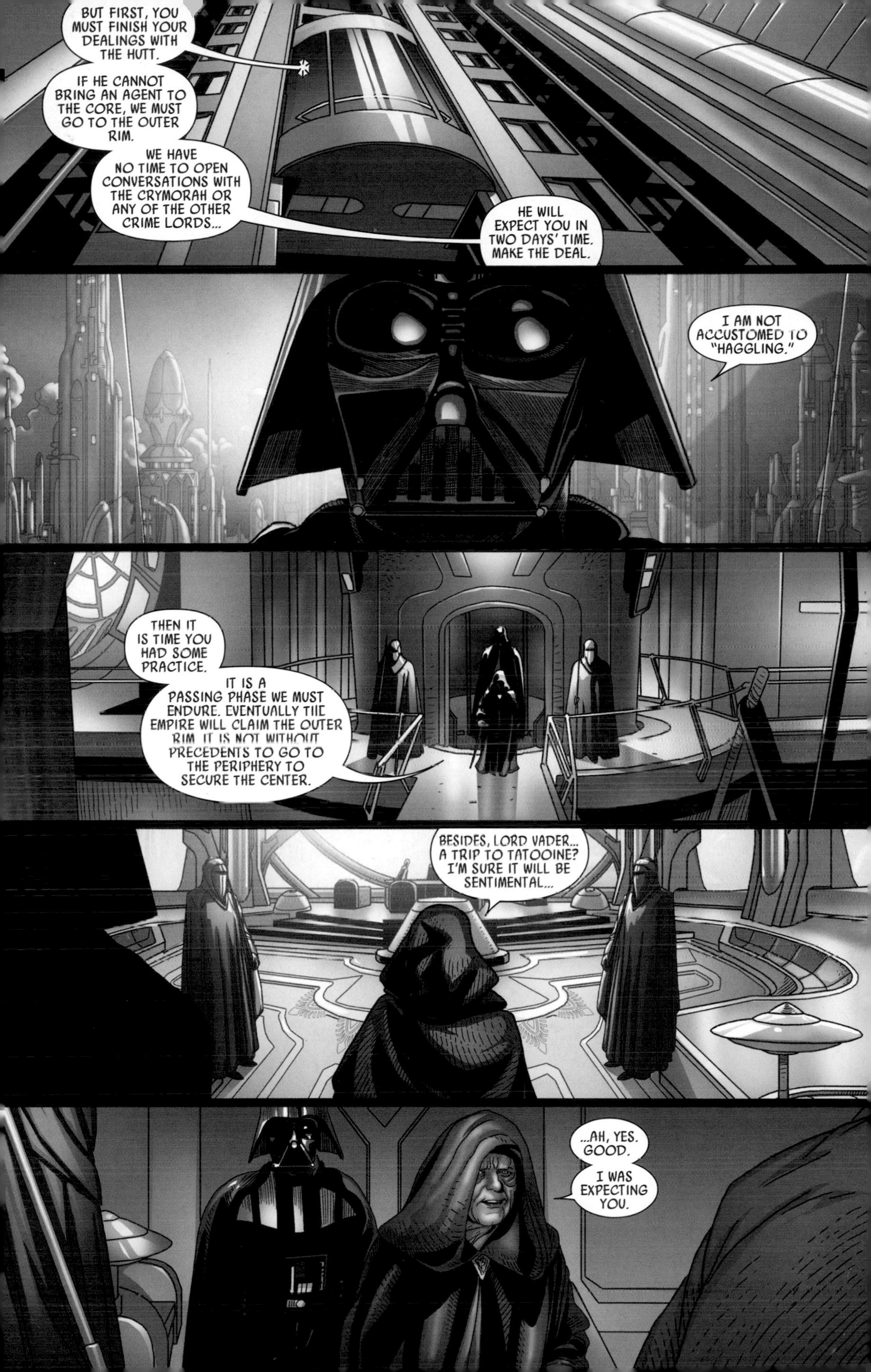
BUT FIRST, YOU MUST FINISH YOUR DEALINGS WITH THE HUTT.
IF HE CANNOT BRING AN AGENT TO THE CORE, WE MUST GO TO THE OUTER RIM.
WE HAVE NO TIME TO OPEN CONVERSATIONS WITH THE CRYMORAH OR ANY OF THE OTHER CRIME LORDS...
HE WILL EXPECT YOU IN TWO DAYS' TIME. MAKE THE DEAL.
I AM NOT ACCUSTOMED TO "HAGGLING."
THEN IT IS TIME YOU HAD SOME PRACTICE.
IT IS A PASSING PHASE WE MUST ENDURE. EVENTUALLY THE EMPIRE WILL CLAIM THE OUTER RIM. IT IS NOT WITHOUT PRECEDENTS TO GO TO THE PERIPHERY TO SECURE THE CENTER.
BESIDES, LORD VADER... A TRIP TO TATOOINE? I'M SURE IT WILL BE SENTIMENTAL...
...AH, YES. GOOD.
I WAS EXPECTING YOU.

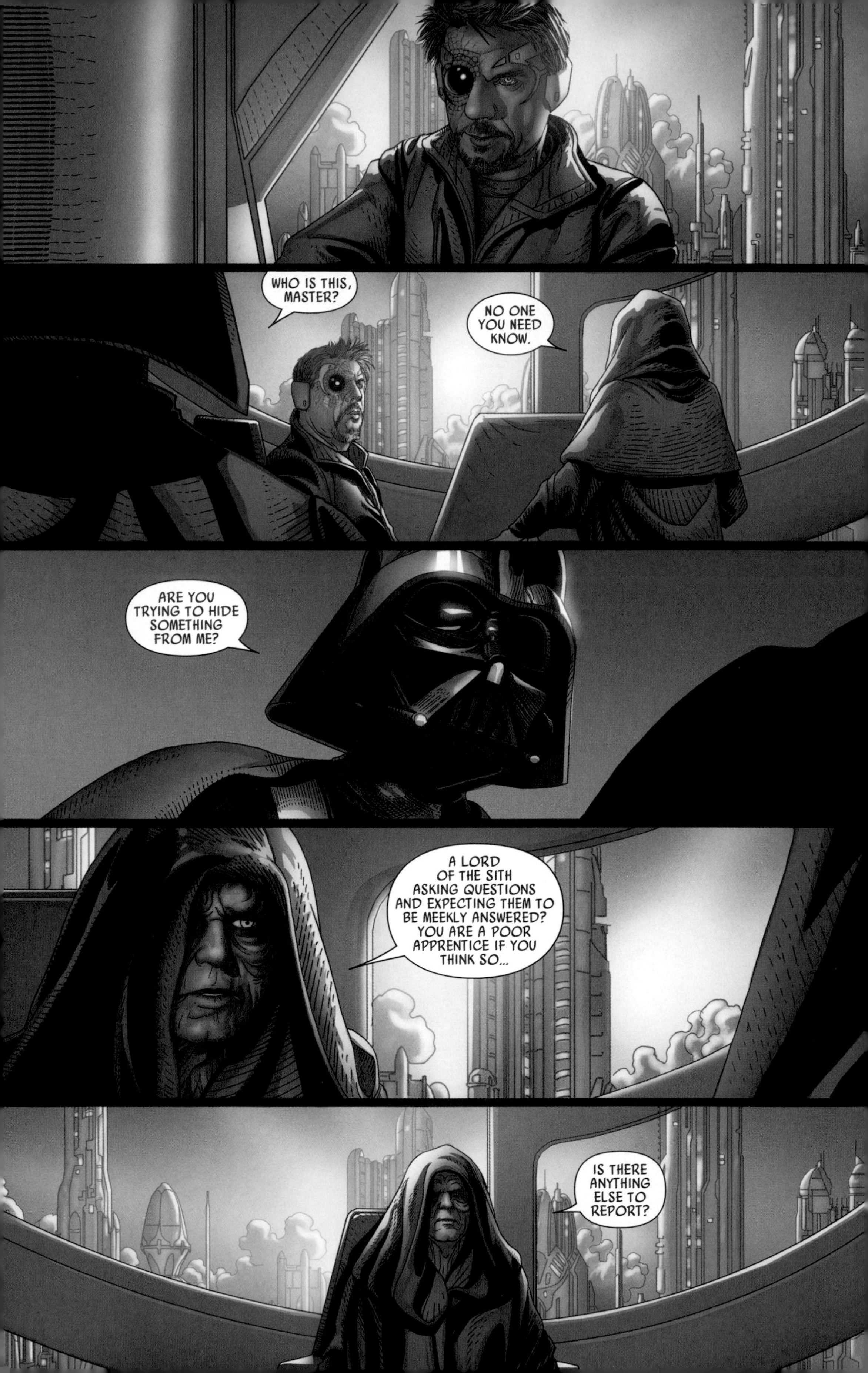
WHO IS THIS, MASTER?
NO ONE YOU NEED KNOW.
ARE YOU TRYING TO HIDE SOMETHING FROM ME?
A LORD OF THE SITH ASKING QUESTIONS AND EXPECTING THEM TO BE MEEKLY ANSWERED? YOU ARE A POOR APPRENTICE IF YOU THINK SO...
IS THERE ANYTHING ELSE TO REPORT?

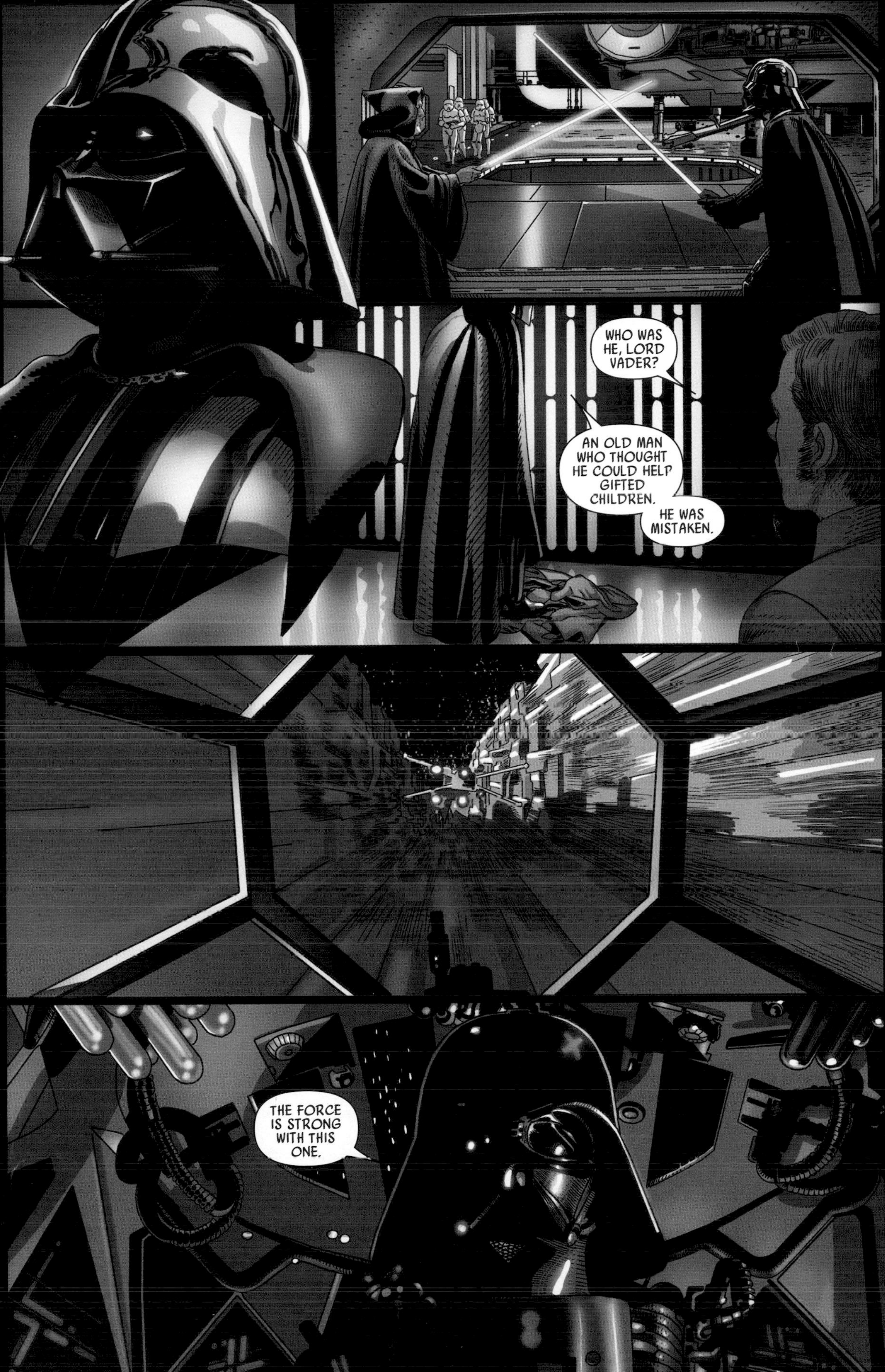
WHO WAS HE, LORD VADER?
AN OLD MAN WHO THOUGHT HE COULD HELP GIFTED CHILDREN.
HE WAS MISTAKEN.
THE FORCE IS STRONG WITH THIS ONE.

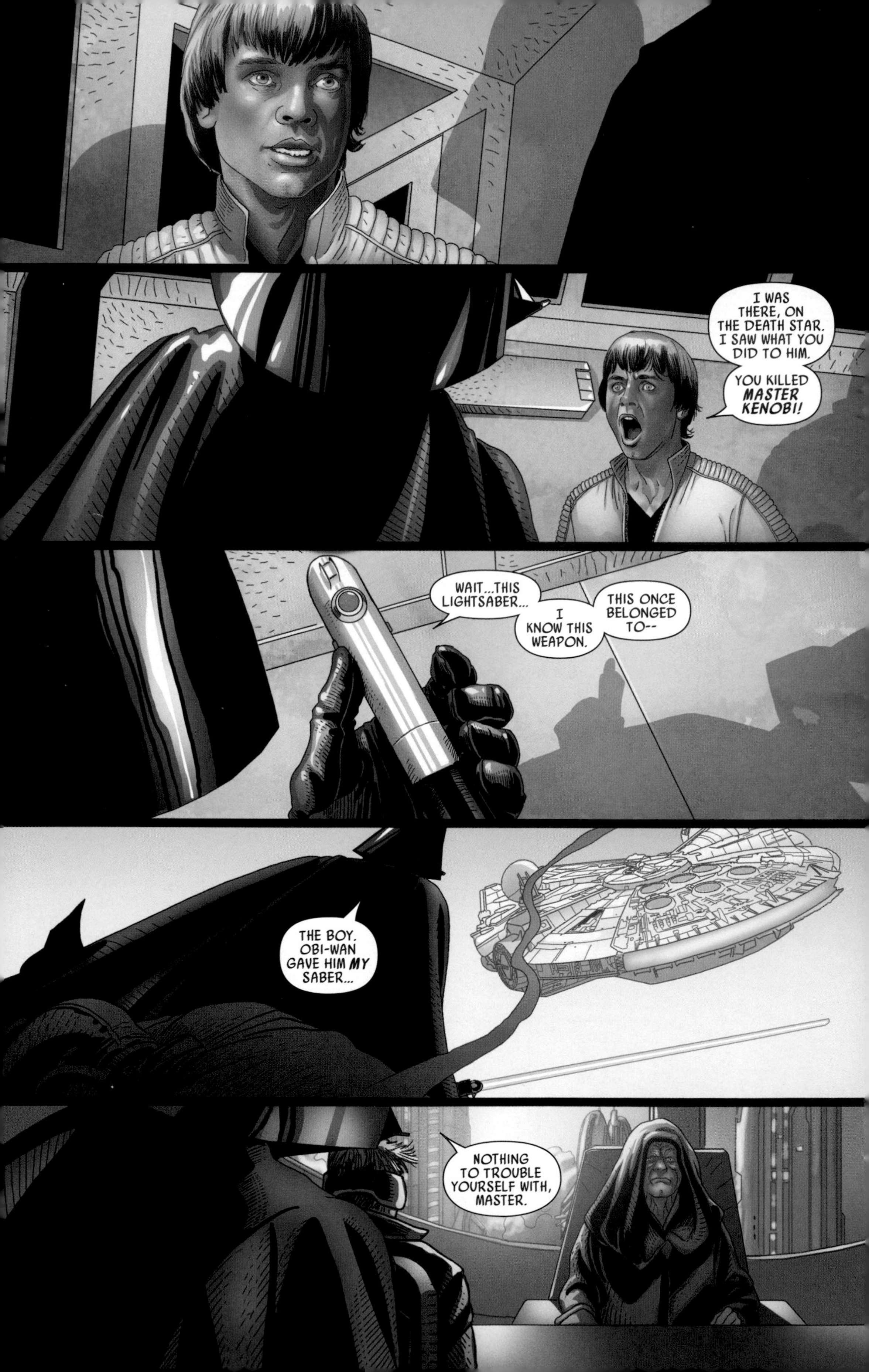
I WAS THERE, ON THE DEATH STAR. I SAW WHAT YOU DID TO HIM.
YOU KILLED MASTER KENOBI!
WAIT...THIS LIGHTSABER...
I KNOW THIS WEAPON.
THIS ONCE BELONGED TO--
THE BOY. OBI-WAN GAVE HIM MY SABER...
NOTHING TO TROUBLE YOURSELF WITH, MASTER.

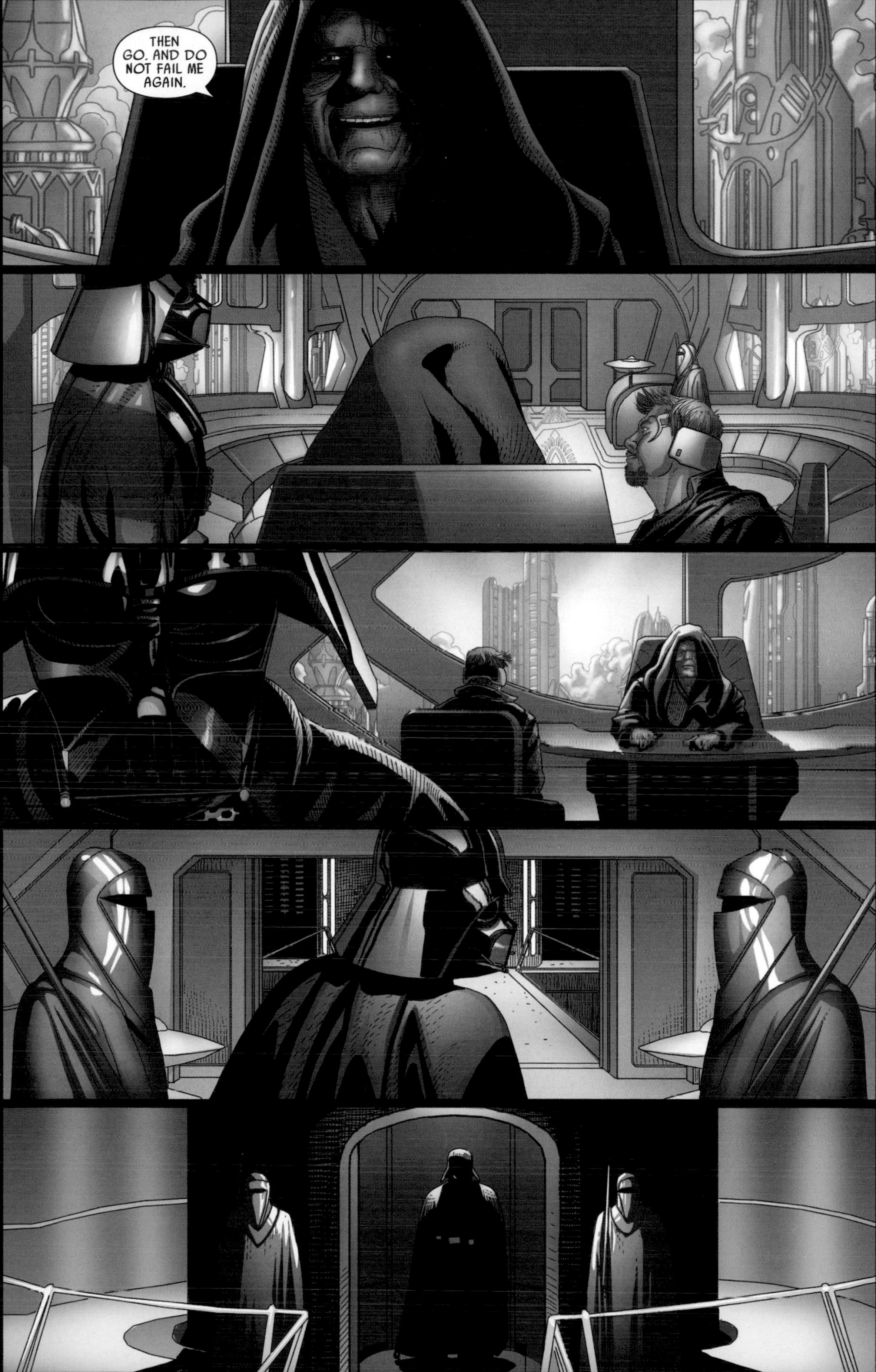
THEN GO. AND DO NOT FAIL ME AGAIN.

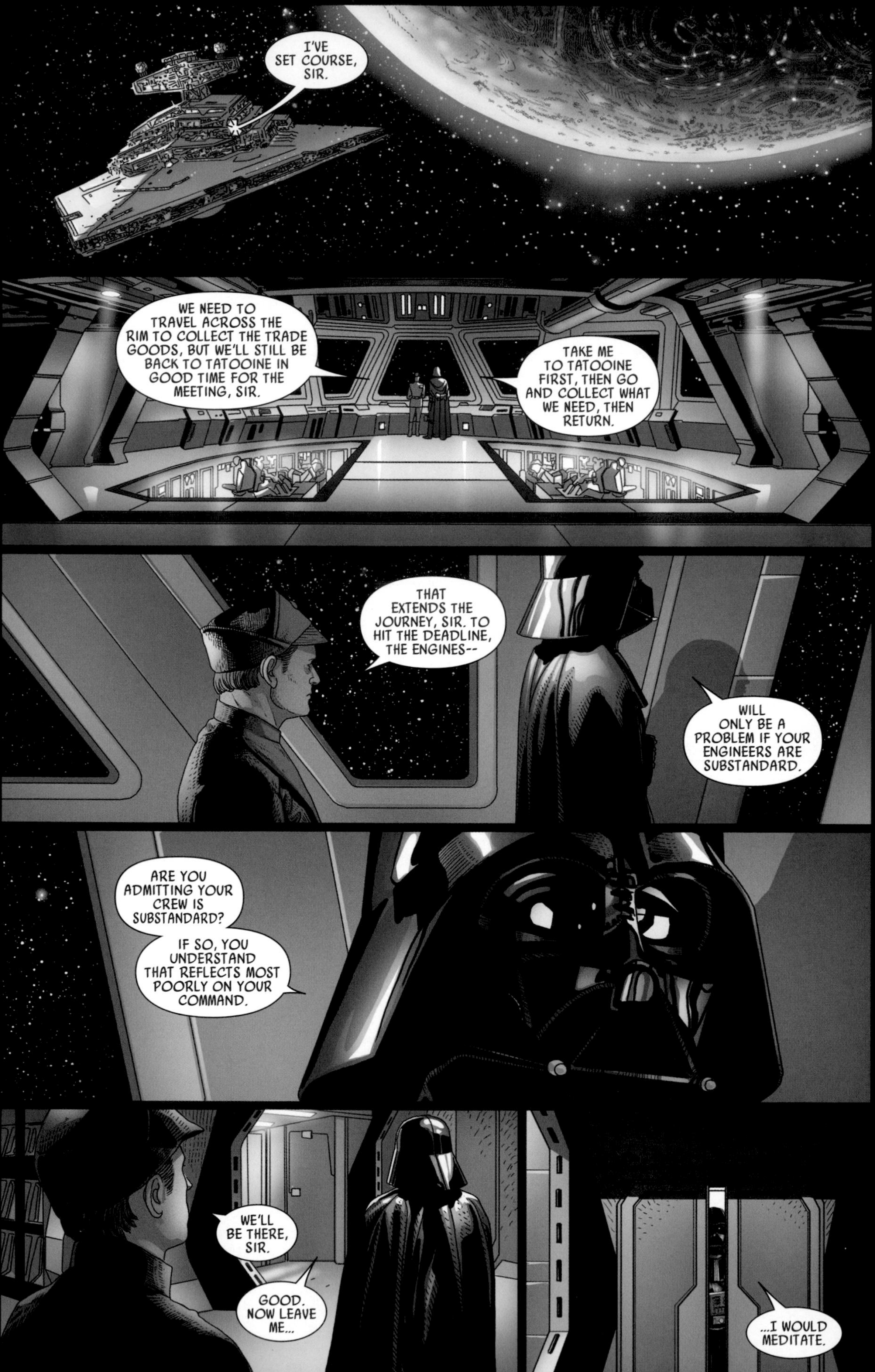
I'VE SET COURSE, SIR.
WE NEED TO TRAVEL ACROSS THE RIM TO COLLECT THE TRADE GOODS, BUT WE'LL STILL BE BACK TO TATOOINE IN GOOD TIME FOR THE MEETING, SIR.
TAKE ME TO TATOOINE FIRST, THEN GO AND COLLECT WHAT WE NEED, THEN RETURN.
THAT EXTENDS THE JOURNEY, SIR. TO HIT THE DEADLINE, THE ENGINES--
WILL ONLY BE A PROBLEM IF YOUR ENGINEERS ARE SUBSTANDARD.
ARE YOU ADMITTING YOUR CREW IS SUBSTANDARD?
IF SO, YOU UNDERSTAND THAT REFLECTS MOST POORLY ON YOUR COMMAND.
WE'LL BE THERE, SIR.
GOOD. NOW LEAVE ME...
...I WOULD MEDITATE.

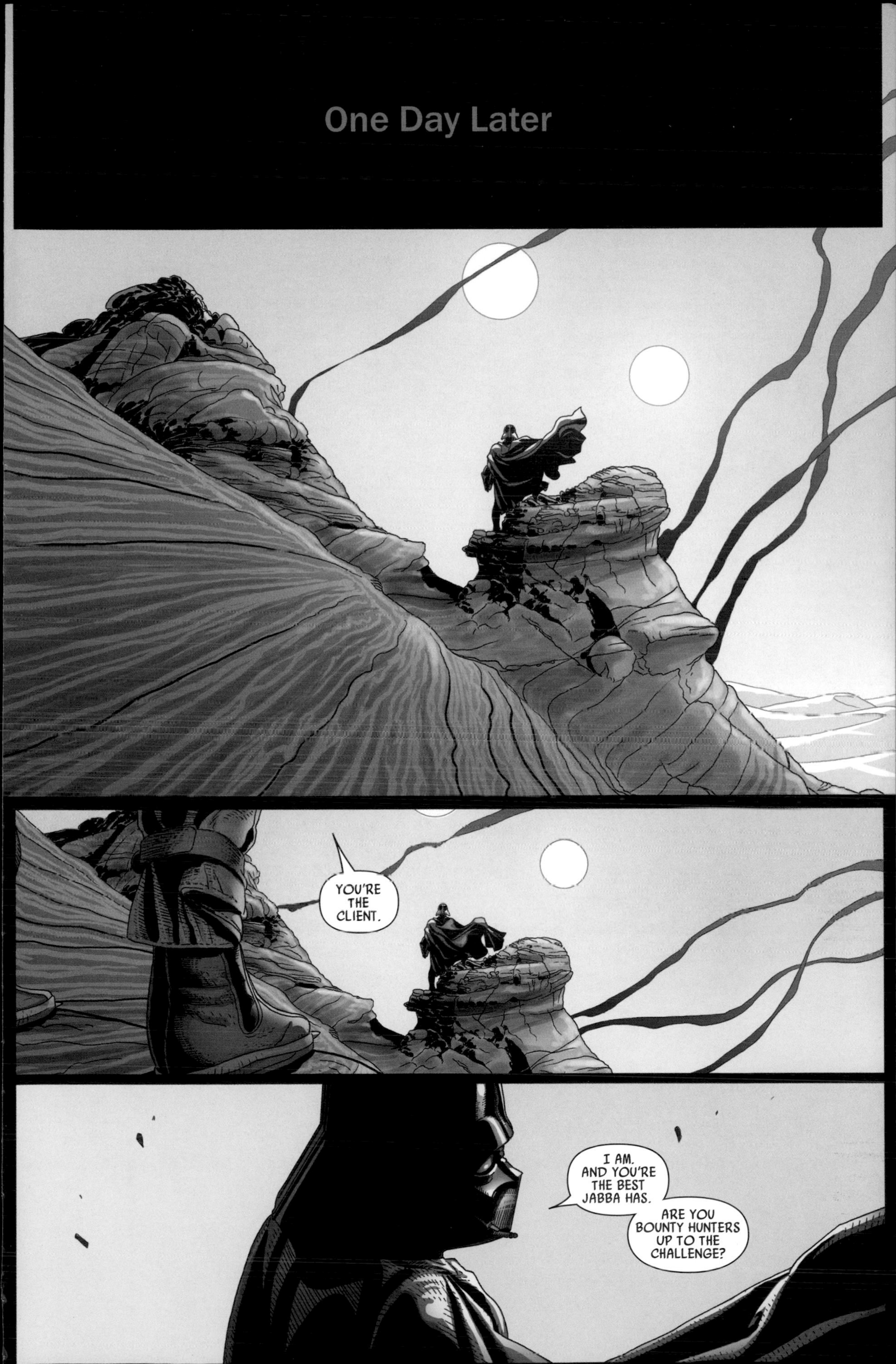
One Day Later
YOU'RE THE CLIENT.
I AM. AND YOU'RE THE BEST JABBA HAS.
ARE YOU BOUNTY HUNTERS UP TO THE CHALLENGE?

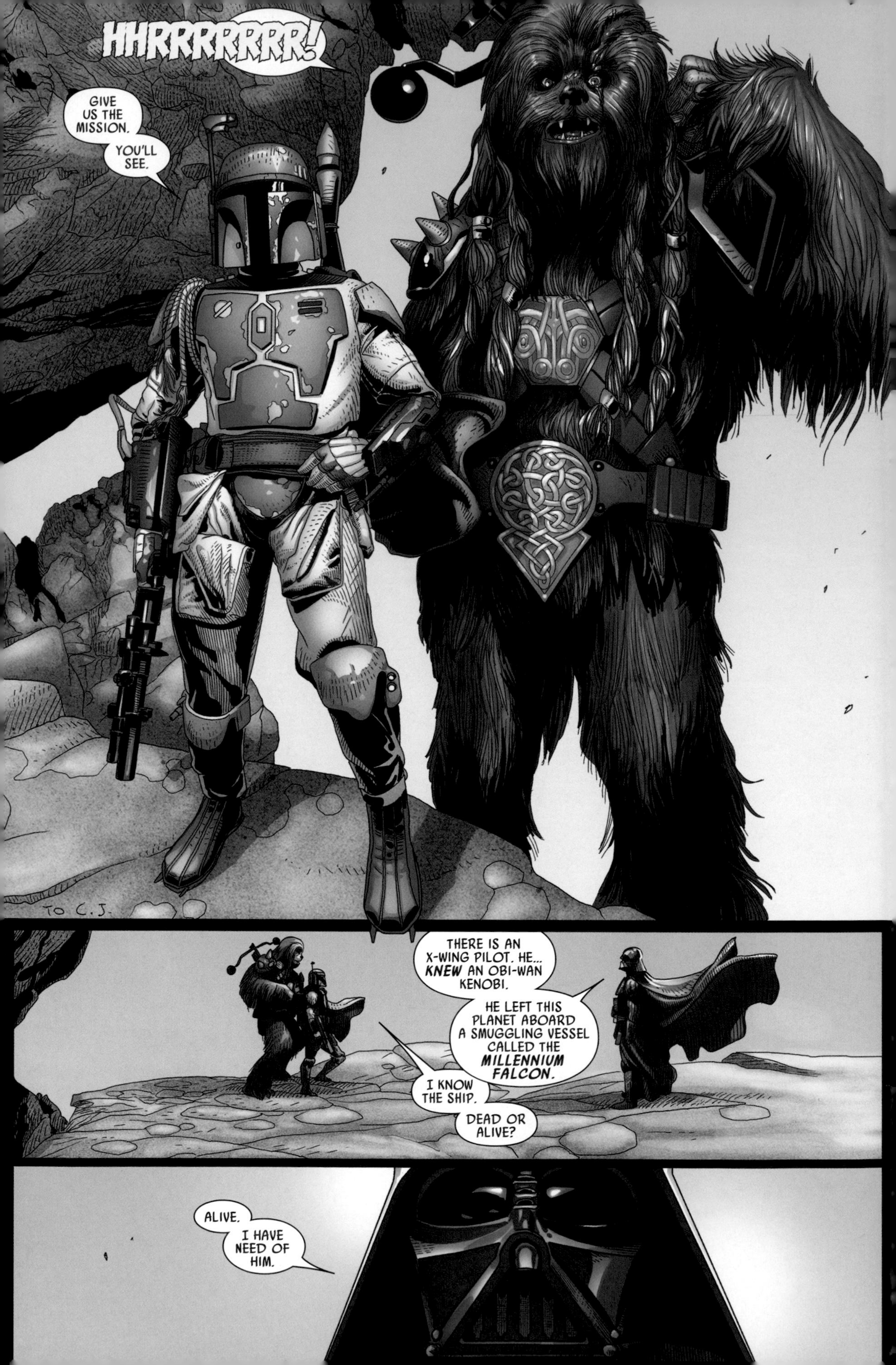
HHRRRRRRR!
GIVE US THE MISSION.
YOU'LL SEE.
TO C.J.
THERE IS AN X-WING PILOT. HE... **KNEW** AN OBI-WAN KENOBI.
HE LEFT THIS PLANET ABOARD A SMUGGLING VESSEL CALLED THE ***MILLENNIUM FALCON***.
I KNOW THE SHIP.
DEAD OR ALIVE?
ALIVE.
I HAVE NEED OF HIM.

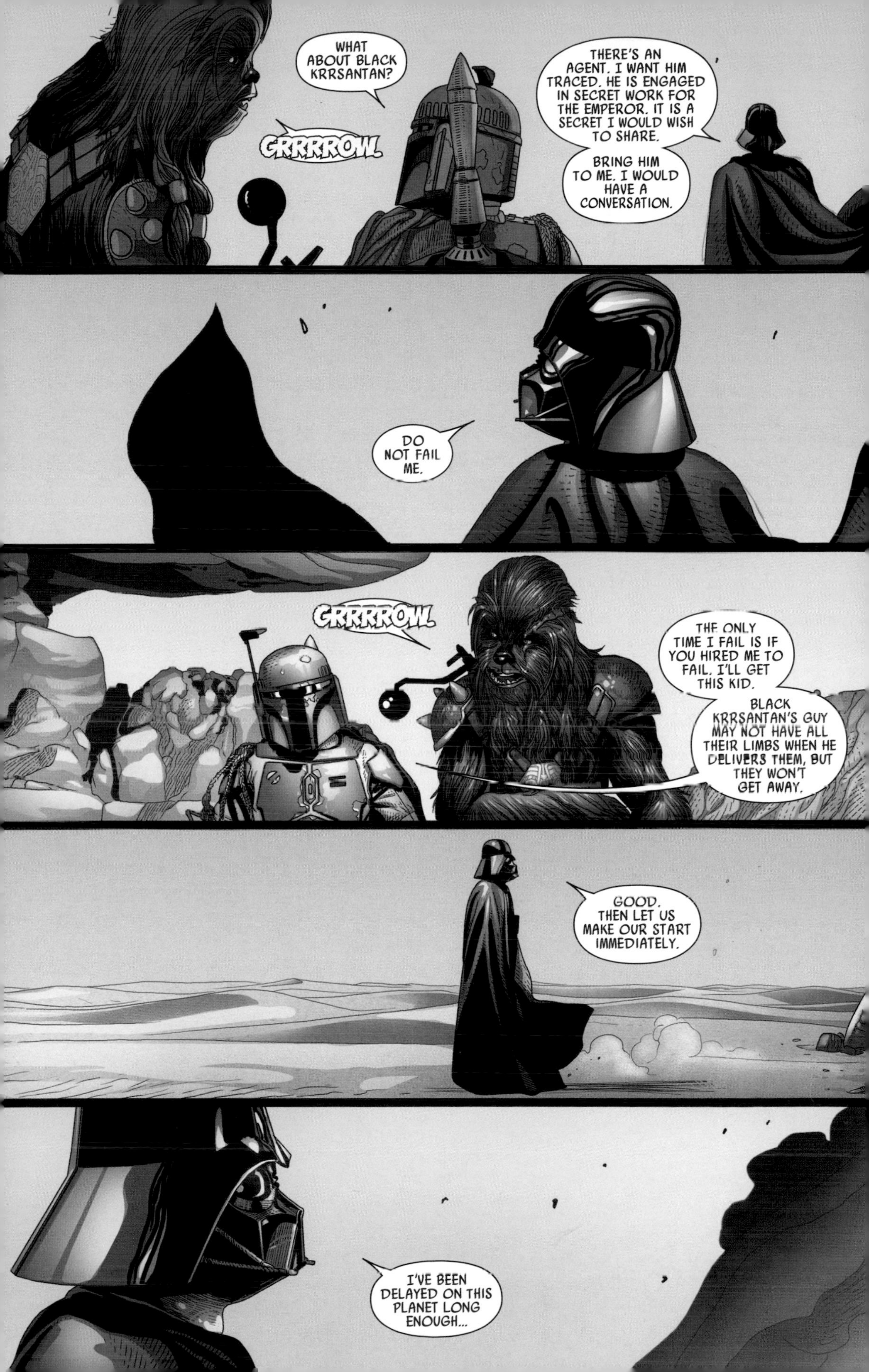
WHAT ABOUT BLACK KRRSANTAN?
GRRRROW.
THERE'S AN AGENT. I WANT HIM TRACED. HE IS ENGAGED IN SECRET WORK FOR THE EMPEROR. IT IS A SECRET I WOULD WISH TO SHARE.
BRING HIM TO ME. I WOULD HAVE A CONVERSATION.
DO NOT FAIL ME.
GRRRROW.
THE ONLY TIME I FAIL IS IF YOU HIRED ME TO FAIL. I'LL GET THIS KID.
BLACK KRRSANTAN'S GUY MAY NOT HAVE ALL THEIR LIMBS WHEN HE DELIVERS THEM, BUT THEY WON'T GET AWAY.
GOOD. THEN LET US MAKE OUR START IMMEDIATELY.
I'VE BEEN DELAYED ON THIS PLANET LONG ENOUGH...

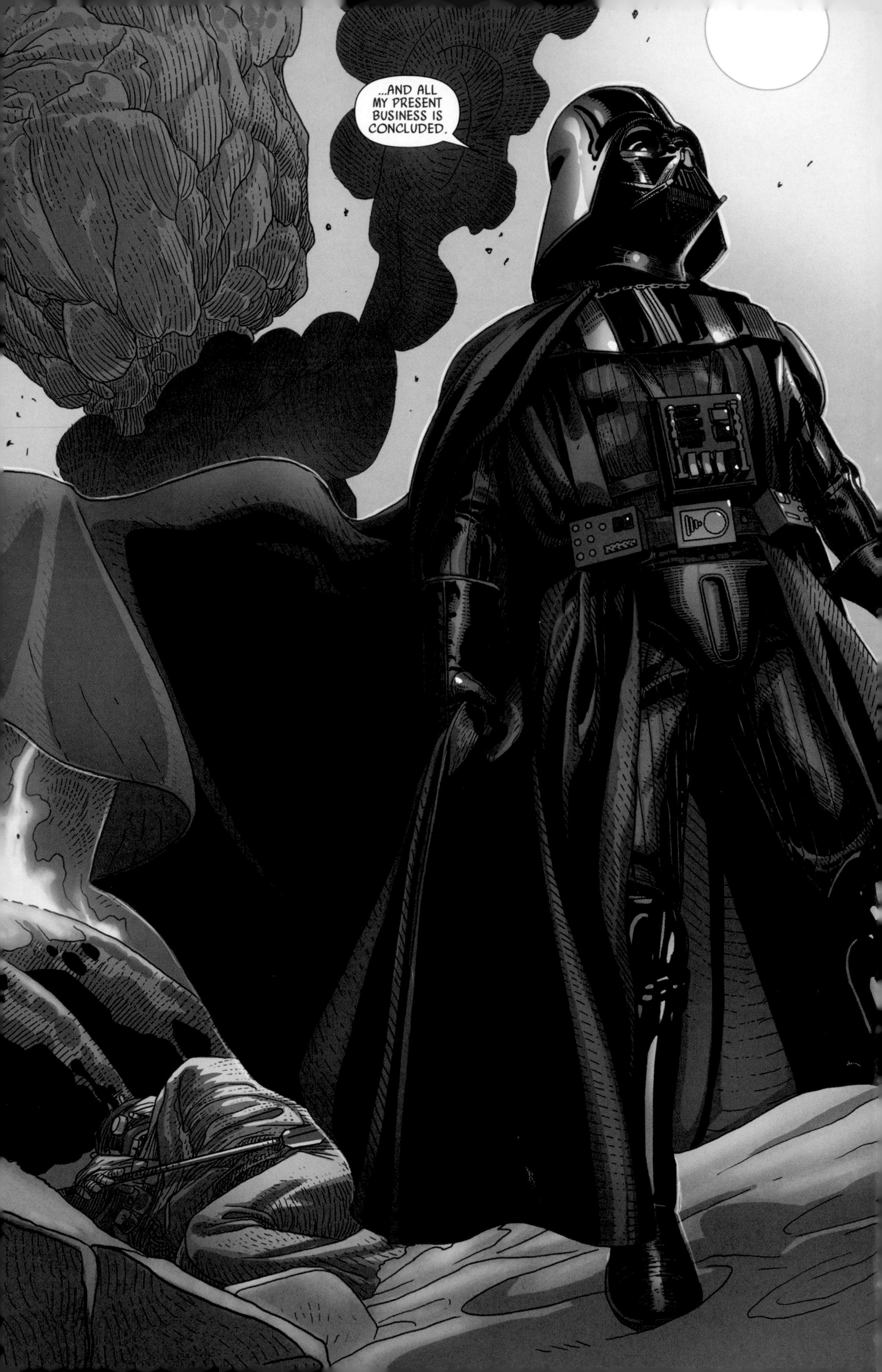
...AND ALL MY PRESENT BUSINESS IS CONCLUDED.

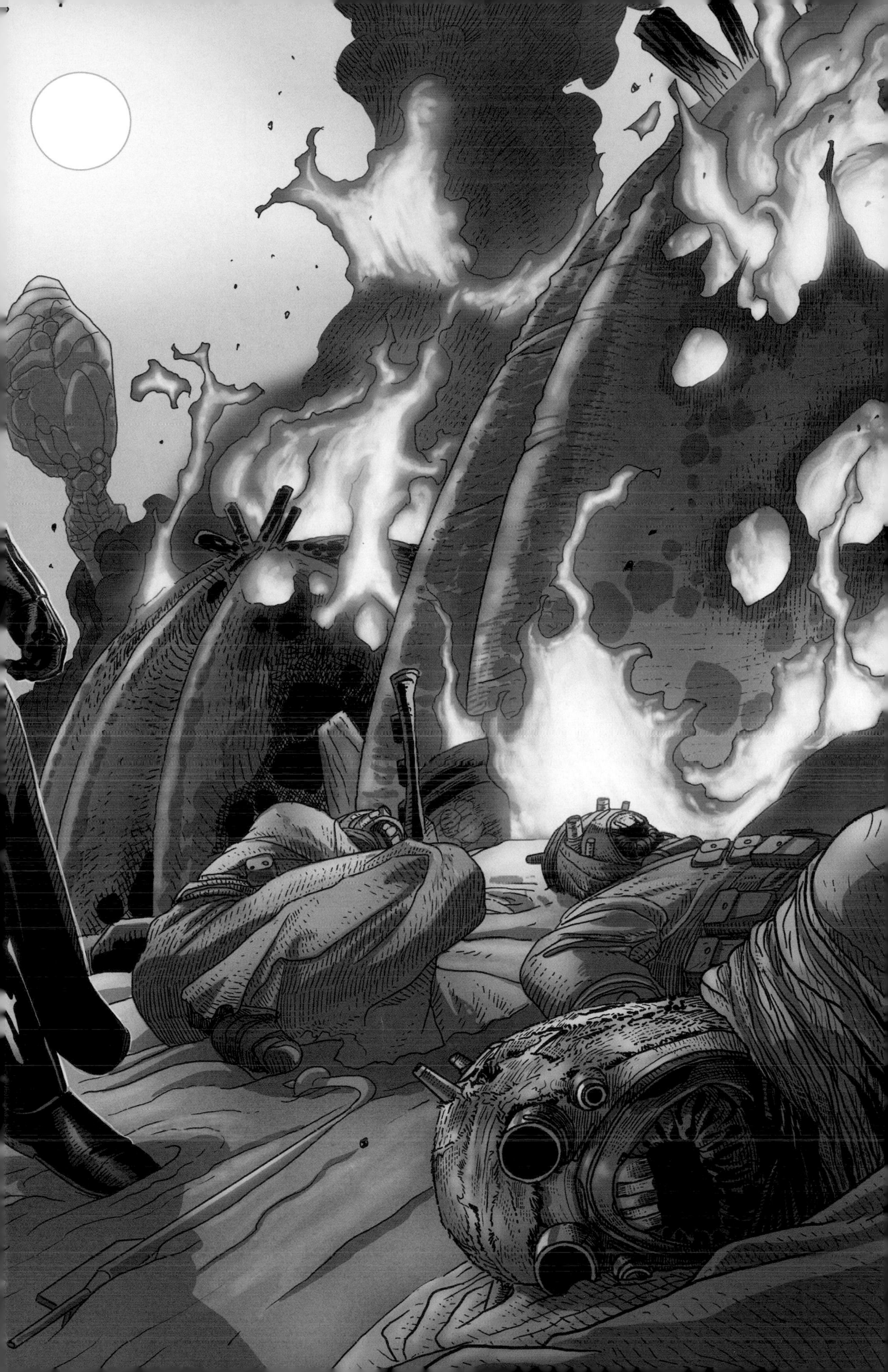

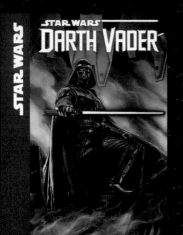
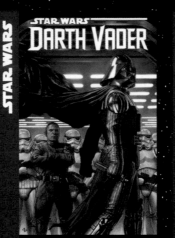
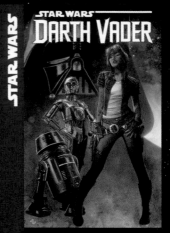

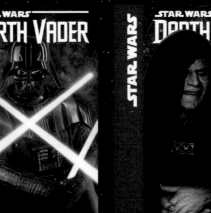